The image ... **face, even** ... **closed.**

Carrie with the sun shining on her dazzling copper-colored hair the first day he saw her.

Carrie with her face over a hot stove, the steam curling her hair around her face.

Carrie in the hot springs, her whole luscious body pink and warm and so desirable, he felt the ache of longing deep inside him. A desire he feared would be with him for a long, long time.

Carrie in bed with him, her face aglow.

He turned over and buried his face in his pillow. But the images wouldn't stop.

Images of what he'd be losing when he left Alaska forever....

Dear Reader,

Happy New Year! January is an exciting month here at Harlequin American Romance. It marks the beginning of a yearlong celebration of our 20th anniversary. Come indulge with us for twelve months of supersatisfying reads by your favorite authors and exciting newcomers, too!

Throughout 2003, we'll be bringing you some not-to-miss miniseries. This month, bestselling author Muriel Jensen inaugurates MILLIONAIRE, MONTANA, our newest in-line continuity, with *Jackpot Baby*. This exciting six-book series is set in a small Montana town whose residents win a forty-million-dollar lottery jackpot. But winning a fortune comes with a price and no one's life will ever be the same again.

Next, *Commander's Little Surprise*, the latest book in Mollie Molay's GROOMS IN UNIFORM series, is a must-read secret-baby and reunion romance with a strong hero you won't be able to resist. Victoria Chancellor premieres her new A ROYAL TWIST miniseries in which a runaway prince and his horse-wrangling look-alike switch places. Don't miss *The Prince's Cowboy Double*, the first book in this delightful duo. Finally, when a small Alaskan town desperately needs a doctor, there's only one man who can do the job, in *Under Alaskan Skies* by Carol Grace.

So come join in the celebrating and start your year off right—by reading all four Harlequin American Romance books!

Melissa Jeglinski
Associate Senior Editor
Harlequin American Romance

UNDER ALASKAN SKIES
Carol Grace

HARLEQUIN®

TORONTO • NEW YORK • LONDON
AMSTERDAM • PARIS • SYDNEY • HAMBURG
STOCKHOLM • ATHENS • TOKYO • MILAN • MADRID
PRAGUE • WARSAW • BUDAPEST • AUCKLAND

ISBN 0-373-16956-6

UNDER ALASKAN SKIES

This edition published by arrangement with Harlequin Books S.A.

® and TM are trademarks of the publisher. Trademarks indicated with ® are registered in the United States Patent and Trademark Office, the Canadian Trade Marks Office and in other countries.

Visit us at www.eHarlequin.com

Printed in U.S.A.

ABOUT THE AUTHOR

Carol Grace has always been interested in travel and living abroad. She spent her junior year of college in France and toured the world, working on the hospital ship HOPE. She and her husband spent the first year and a half of their marriage in Iran, where they both taught English. Then, with their toddler daughter, they lived in Algeria for two years. For Carol, writing is another way of making her life exciting. Her office is her mountaintop home, which overlooks the Pacific Ocean. She lives there with her inventor husband, their daughter, who just graduated from college, and their teenage son.

Books by Carol Grace

HARLEQUIN AMERICAN ROMANCE
836—FAMILY TREE
956—UNDER ALASKAN SKIES

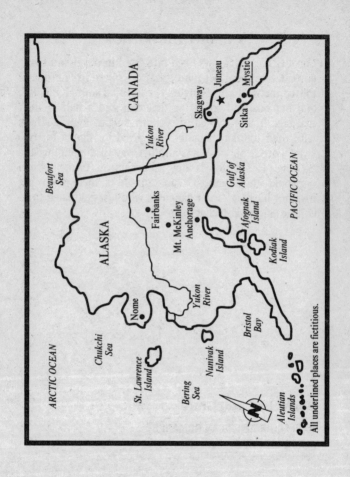

Chapter One

Matt Baker inhaled the damp fresh air from the upper deck of the cruise ship. Up early that morning, before his parents and the other members of their party, he relished the quiet after an evening of dining and dancing, celebrating his parents' fiftieth wedding anniversary in the first-class lounge. Along the shore of Alaska's Inside Passage, the gray-green water lapped at the roots of the forested slopes. Above them, tall mountains loomed in the cool-gray sky. The ship was heading for the small town of Tongass where it would dock for the day, disgorging hundreds of passengers to swarm all over town, filling the curio shops or boarding buses for sightseeing out of town.

In the distance he heard the drone of a single-engine prop plane. Lifting his binoculars, he trained his eyes in the direction of the sound. A small float-plane was approaching. Not an unusual sight. The towns along the Inside Passage, like Tongass, Juneau, Ketchikan and Sitka, were located along Alaska's Marine Highway, accessible only by air or water. There were no roads to most cities or villages in these remote areas of Alaska.

He imagined a logger inside the small plane, coming into town for some R&R at the local saloon or a pilot arriving to pick up sightseers, taking them out to view a glacier up close or to a river where bears pulled salmon out of the rushing waters. He leaned against the polished brass railing. As the cruise ship approached the dock, he kept his eyes on the floatplane.

Matt felt a stab of envy for the pilot. For what? For his freedom to go wherever he wanted? For the thrill of flying over some of the world's greatest scenery? For his ability to leave the earth below and all his problems behind? He shook his head. He had no reason to envy anyone.

The floatplane's engine idled and it slowed to land in the water a quarter mile from the docks, then taxied in on two pontoons, plowing a wake behind it. Matt hurried to the forward deck for a better look at the plane. He was curious to see who the pilot was and how he would tie up. It couldn't be easy to maneuver the craft next to the dock. But he did it. Slowing the engine, the plane sidled up neatly to the pier, a slim figure in a jumpsuit gracefully jumped out, threw a rope around a post, secured it and did the same with another post.

Just then a ray of early-morning sunshine burst threw a cloud and sent a shaft of light across the harbor, outlining the pilot and his craft. Quickly adjusting his binoculars Matt realized with a start that the pilot was not a he. It was a woman, a woman with red hair gleaming like copper in the sunlight. A woman whose jumpsuit couldn't conceal her generous curves. As he watched, she turned slowly, as if she felt his eyes on her, and tilted her head in his direction.

When her gaze met his, he almost dropped his binoculars. He didn't know her. He'd never seen her before. He'd never seen anybody like her before. And yet there was something about her. Something that set his pulse racing and riveted his attention.

Who are you? Where did you come from? What are you doing here? The questions ran through his head nonstop.

"Matt, where have you been? I've been looking all over for you." The voice of Mira Lipton, the daughter of his parents' best friends, startled him.

"Just watching our ship dock," he said, reluctantly turning his back on the woman on the dock. It wasn't really much of a lie. His intention had been just that. To watch the giant cruise ship pull in. Until the little floatplane distracted him. He snapped his binoculars into their case.

"My parents and yours have already gone to the dining room for breakfast," Mira said. "But I wanted to wait for you." She smiled up at him, and tucked her arm in his as they headed toward the main deck, reminding him that she'd not only been waiting to have breakfast with him, she'd been waiting for him to propose to her for a long time. He didn't know why he hadn't. They'd known and liked each other for years. But up till now he'd had some excellent excuses. Medical school, then rotations in the various specialties. Twenty-four-hour workdays. An upcoming internship in plastic surgery. A minuscule income to support a wife.

But now, now that he was on the downhill slope

of a long and expensive education, with a lucrative career ahead of him, he had no more real excuses. Why should he want any? To quote his mother, "Mira really is a lovely girl and nobody would be surprised if after all these years, you finally decided to get married." And yet...and yet...

"So...what do you think?" she asked.

"About what?"

"You haven't heard a word I've said," she chided gently. Too gently. Sometimes he wished she'd stamp her foot and insist that he pay attention to her. Or demand to know what his intentions were. But then he'd have to say he had no such intentions. That he had too much else to think about right now. Such as the internship at a major teaching hospital and his father's health.

"I asked if you were bringing your camera to the bald eagle preserve or if I should bring mine. They say we fly right over their nests."

"Fly?" he said, suddenly alert.

"In a helicopter."

"Oh, right." For a moment he had pictured himself sitting next to the red-haired woman in her small plane, her copper-colored hair brushing his shoulder as she banked her plane over the eagle reserve for a view of the rare birds. Deliberately he shut off any such image. Ridiculous, daydreaming about a strange woman who was probably a forest ranger married to a lighthouse keeper when he himself had a perfectly fine available woman at his side. He studied Mira's profile as they headed toward the dining room. Pale-blond hair brushed her cheek. Blue eyes and delicate features. She was not only pretty, she was intelligent and came from a similar background. Their parents were best friends. What more could he want? He didn't know. He just knew that deep down there was more. That he wanted to have it all. He just didn't know what "all" was.

CARRIE PORTER STOOD at the foot of the gangway, shifting her weight from one foot to the other as she stared up at the gleaming white cruise ship. She willed someone to walk down and remove the gate that stood between her and the entrance to the ship and the person she desperately needed to see. Finally an officer in a blue uniform came walking toward her, a stern look on his angular features.

"I'm sorry, no visitors allowed onboard. We'll be disembarking in a few minutes."

"I have to see the ship's doctor," she said. "It's an emergency."

"The ship's doctor is only available for passengers. I can take a message to him if you want."

"I can't wait. I have to see him now. It's urgent."

"Isn't there a doctor here in town?" he asked.

"He's down with the flu. I talked to him on the phone. He's the one who suggested I try the ship."

"Sorry. What about Ketchikan, Haines or Sitka?"

"Yes, they're next on my list, but first I need to try the ship's doctor. At least I need to ask him, then if he won't come...."

"What's wrong with you?" he asked with a frown. "You don't look sick to me."

She shook her head impatiently. "It's not for me. A boy in my village is hurt badly. He needs to see a doctor. I've got a plane, but I can't...I can't..." She clenched her jaw to keep from screaming or crying in frustration, which wouldn't help her cause at all. She must keep calm, reasonable, but she must find somebody. Now.

She took a deep breath. "I can't go back without finding a doctor," she continued. "Please, could I just have a word with him? Five minutes?"

The ship's officer stared at her for a long moment. Finally he shrugged and unlocked the gate. Once inside the luxury vessel, he gave her directions to the infirmary. Two decks down, turn right at the shore excursion desk.

The ship's doctor was old. He was sweet. When he heard her story he was also sympathetic. He agreed that the situation was serious and she needed a medic. But there was nothing he could do. His contract required him to stay on the ship.

"Wait a minute," he said, scratching his bald head. "There's a doctor aboard. Two of them in fact. Father and son. Came down and introduced themselves. Baker was their name. Now, I don't know if they'd be willing to go with you. They're on vacation you know. You say you've got a plane?"

Carrie's heart skipped a beat. Two of them. Surely one of the two... "Yes, a plane. We're only a half hour away. How can I get in touch with the doctors?"

The kindly old G.P. called their cabins, and after what seemed to her an eternity of pacing back and forth in the waiting room, along with several sick crew members, two men walked in. One was probably in his sixties, wearing slacks and a windbreaker, the other, thirty-something in jeans and a jacket.

Dark eyes, strong features. They were obviously father and son.

She rushed to meet them before they'd barely come through the door. "Dr. Baker?" she asked, her eyes traveling from one to the other.

"Eugene Baker," said the older man.

"Matt Baker," said the younger doctor.

She didn't know which one to approach first. Eugene, the older, silver-haired, dignified one or Matt, the one who looked like he came right out of central casting—tall with dark hair, brown eyes and an air of competence. More than competence. More like, I'm here and everything's going to be all right. They called it a bedside manner, even though there wasn't even a bed in sight. She had the strange feeling she'd seen him before. She probably had. Because, although he wasn't wearing a white lab coat, he definitely belonged on TV in a show like *E.R.* or *Chicago Hope* or…or a soap opera like *General Hospital.* He was altogether too good-looking to be real. Forget the looks. Forget everything but convincing one of these Drs. Baker to come with her back to the small village of Mystic.

She took a deep breath. "My name is Carrie Porter. I'm from a village about a half hour by floatplane from here. There's been an accident and we badly need a doctor. You've got to come. You just have to." The words gushed out faster than oil from the Alaska pipeline.

"Calm down, Ms. Porter," the older doctor said. "Surely there are local doctors who could help you."

"I called around but didn't find anybody. I could have kept calling, but I didn't have the time. Every minute counts. When I heard the cruise ship was due in port, I just got in my plane and headed this way, hoping, praying…'' She looked at Dr. Matt Baker, got lost in the depths of his dark-brown eyes for a moment. She was looking for sympathy and she saw it. She saw that and something else. Something she couldn't identify. Emboldened, she rushed on before he had a chance to say no. ''I know you're on vacation. I know I'm imposing but…''

''Why don't you tell us what the problem is,'' Matt said. The sound of his deep voice made her feel better. She knew in an instant if she was sick she'd want him to take care of her. Just being in his presence made her feel better. If she had a choice, she'd choose him. But she couldn't afford to be choosy. She'd take either one. Once they realized how serious the situation was, they'd be willing to help. They just had to.

''Yes, of course.'' She should have told them immediately what the problem was. How could they agree to go with her when they didn't even know what had happened. She made an effort to clear her mind and speak slowly. ''This morning a young boy in our town was riding on his dad's three-wheel all-terrain vehicle. It tipped over and threw him into a post. He landed on his back and he can't move from the waist down. He's in terrible pain. He must have broken something. I don't know much about medicine but I know that it's serious and that he needs to see somebody right away. I didn't know what to do except keep him still. I would have flown him out but everyone I talked to said not to move him. Now I'm afraid—''

''Where is he now?'' Matt asked

"He's at home in bed. Oh, you mean where— He…we…live in a small village called Mystic at the tip of a fjord."

"You say he's paralyzed?" Eugene Baker asked.

"Partly, yes."

Matt and his father exchanged glances. She didn't like the way they looked at each other.

"You shouldn't have moved him at all," the older doctor said sternly.

"But we couldn't leave him out in the rain and the cold," she said.

"Is he having trouble breathing?" Matt asked.

"No, I don't think so."

"Lucky he didn't land on his head. He could be paraplegic. There's no telling how serious the injury is without a good workup," Eugene said.

"Not likely to get one where he is," Matt said. "You say you have no doctor in town?"

She shook her head. "We had a nurse but she left last year."

"What do you do in emergencies?" Matt asked.

"Try to get advice by phone. Call the med evac people if it's serious."

"At the very least he ought to get started on steroids to reduce the swelling," Eugene suggested to his son.

Matt nodded. "What about putting him in traction."

"Probably. But what can you do without braces or weights or a harness?"

"I have splints in my cabinet here," said a voice from behind them. "And a cervical collar. In case that would help."

Carrie and the two doctors turned around. Neither of them realized the ship's doctor had joined them in the waiting room and had obviously heard most of the conversation.

"You've got a supply of steroids, of course," Matt said.

The old G.P. nodded.

Carrie was afraid to speak. Afraid to ask again, Will you come? Will you come now? Afraid to push too hard. Afraid to upset the momentum, though she was sure time was of the essence. As three medics stood there looking at each other while the precious minutes ticked away, something in her head snapped. She lost her cool.

"Someone has to come. I don't care which one of you," she said heatedly. "I have my plane here at the dock. I'll have you back, I promise, before the ship leaves port today. But we have to leave now."

The men looked at her, obviously surprised at her change in attitude. She was no longer asking, she was telling. She didn't care what they thought of her, unless there was a danger of scaring them off. The older man turned to his son.

"I'll go, Matt," Eugene said. "There may be nothing I can do on my own, without a CAT scan, an MRI or an X ray, but the least I can do is take a look at him."

"No, Dad. You stay here. I can handle it," Matt said firmly. "We can't have you isolated somewhere just in case..."

Carrie's head turned from father to son. Not only did she have one volunteer, they both wanted to come. She couldn't believe it. She felt like jumping up and down and grabbing Matt's arm and running down the gangway to the dock before he changed his mind. He said he'd go. They both said they'd go. At last, she'd found someone.

"You'll miss the helicopter tour of the bald eagle preserve," his father said. "But if you're going, she's right, you'd better leave now. The time between the accident and treatment is critical."

"I can take you over the preserve," Carrie said to Matt. "We'll pass right by it." She'd take him over glaciers and gorges and waterfalls. She'd give him a tour of Alaska like nobody had ever seen. Anything. She was so grateful her heart was spilling over.

"See, Dad? I won't miss a thing," Matt said calmly. "And I'll be back by evening, right?"

"Yes, right," Carrie said. "Oh, thank you. I can't tell you how relieved I am."

"Better take along extra supplies, drug samples and equipment, if the doctor here can spare them," the elder Dr. Baker said, with a nod at the ship's doctor. "You never know what you may run into. I just hope you can do something for the boy. He may be paralyzed for good, there's no telling, and you won't be able to do a thing about it, except raise false expectations. But you've got to try."

"I will," Matt said. "If I can do anything at all to help, it will be worth taking a chance."

Carrie held her breath and closed her eyes so she wouldn't look at her watch again. *Let's go. Let's go,* she said to herself.

"He's right," Matt said to Carrie. "You have to realize I can't perform miracles. It may be he's permanently paralyzed. On the other hand, he might get well by himself without me. But I'll do what I can.''

''That's all I ask,'' Carrie said. ''Now if you're ready…''

''Let me see what the doctor has that I can take with me,'' Matt said, following the ship's doctor into his office.

Matt's father sat on a bench, but Carrie was too nervous to hold still. She paced back and forth in the waiting room.

''You're a brave young lady flying around these parts,'' Eugene said. ''I assume you have a reliable pilot with you.''

''I'm the pilot.''

Eugene raised his eyebrows in surprise.

She hoped she looked capable of flying a plane and trustworthy, dependable and reliable. After a long, searching look, he pressed his lips together and nodded, no doubt wishing he'd known this when he'd volunteered to go into the bush. Now his son was flying off into a remote region with a woman pilot. Men of his generation were often surprised at her occupation. Heavens, men of almost any generation were surprised when she showed up to pick up the freight, especially if they were expecting her father. She wondered what Matt's reaction would be. Maybe she should have told them this before she asked if they'd come.

''You're fortunate you found us,'' Eugene said. ''My son is a fine doctor. He'll do whatever he can to help you. He's just starting an internship in plastic surgery with a brilliant career ahead of him. He has everything it takes, courage, intelligence, drive and ambition. I'm very proud of him." He beamed as he spoke of his son's abilities.

"You should be," Carrie murmured. She could almost hear her own father touting her to friends and neighbors. It used to embarrass her to hear him describe how well she'd done at school. What a good pilot she was. How she could handle the plane as well if not better than he could. It was a universal trait, bragging about one's children. Dr. Baker seemed to have plenty to brag about.

"Of course, it would be better if you'd found a local doctor," Eugene continued, "someone who could follow up on the patient and give the boy long-term care he needs."

"I know. I wish we had more doctors up here. I appreciate your both volunteering to step in like this at the last minute."

Ten minutes later Matt was on the dock, carrying a bag filled with all the emergency equipment and medicine the ship's doctor could spare. He was standing next to the floatplane he'd observed such a short time ago. If he had been told he would be taking off with a stunning redheaded pilot that morning, he wouldn't have believed it possible. He thought he'd be taking off for a bird's eye view of the local scenery in a sight-seeing helicopter, instead he was going on a mission with a flying angel.

The look in her lovely luminous eyes, the tremor in her lower lip, the catch in her voice all combined to make it nearly impossible for anybody to turn her down. But even if she'd been old and ugly, somebody's gray-haired grandmother in army surplus overalls and combat boots, he still would have gone. He was a doctor and someone was sick. It was as simple as that.

What was not simple were his feelings about the woman. From the first moment he'd spotted her with his binoculars, he'd felt a quickening of his pulse, a flash of recognition. Which was as baffling as it was true. Why her? Why should a big-city doctor feel connected to a bush pilot? It made no sense at all. Was it less than an hour ago he'd envied her, fantasized about flying with her? And now his fantasy had come true. Be careful what you wish for, he cautioned himself. He might be in way over his head and in an impossible situation—both medically and personally. On the other hand, he was used to holding his emotions in check. He had what some might call an over-developed sense of self-discipline.

"I'll need your help," she said after they'd tossed his bag in the plane. She wasn't talking about his medical help this time, she was talking about helping her cast off from the dock. While she started the engine, he followed her directions and untied the ropes, then at the last minute, quickly jumped through the open door and crawled into the jump seat of the plane.

"Good work. Thanks. You're a natural," she said. "Have you done this before?"

He shook his head. He almost said, *But I saw you do it an hour ago.* Ridiculous how her praise made him feel like a hero, all out of proportion to the words she spoke. She was only being polite. It was the smile she gave him that made him feel as light-headed as if he'd had a glass of champagne for breakfast instead of orange juice. He just hoped he could do something beyond casting off, something for the boy.

Fascinated, he watched her rev up the motor, point her tiny plane toward the bay and do her pretakeoff checks. Moving the flaps, pushing on the rudder pedals, throwing switches. He knew plenty of gutsy women. Classmates of his who were training to be surgeons who could wield the knife as skillfully as any male. There were women who blazed the way for others in orthopedics, who'd taken verbal abuse from professors and fellow students. But he didn't know any female pilots. He certainly knew none who looked like this woman. While he watched her go through the motions, she turned on her radio and shook her head as static filled the air.

"The VH won't work till we get airborne," she said. "Above the hills."

He nodded. He watched her hands on the throttle. She had long slender fingers and short fingernails. The roar of the engine filled the air as she accelerated to full power.

He followed her gaze as she looked right and left out the windows to see that the flaps were fully down. She looked like an expert and exuded confidence. Fascinated, he couldn't take his eyes from her. He decided she actually looked like an advertisement from some outdoor magazine in her navy jumpsuit and leather ankle boots. But no photograph could have captured the fire in her eyes when she was determined to get something.

For a moment in the doctor's office he'd had the feeling she would have kidnapped him if he hadn't agreed to go with her. She was that determined. The idea of being kidnapped by her was intriguing and led to all kinds of imaginary scenarios. He hadn't indulged in fantasies since he could remember. He'd been focused on his work for years. By leaving the ship and land behind, he felt as if he'd left another life behind him.

As they taxied out beyond the breakwater, she gunned the engine and the beating of the propeller was so strong the windows and doors rattled. The plane felt so sluggish and heavy in the water he thought they would never get up into the air. But with an even louder roar it began to climb slowly. Slowly but surely they rose into the gray sky. She turned and gave him a dazzling smile and a thumbs-up.

He grinned at her, and their eyes met and held for a long moment. In that moment he knew why people flew small planes. In that space between earth and sky he felt his whole body take off and with a powerful thrust he defied the laws of gravity and became lighter than air. He knew too that if he achieved nothing else this trip, he'd won another smile from Carrie Porter—angel, pilot, goddess, whoever she was.

"Just so you know, I've been flying since I was sixteen," she shouted over the sound of the engine. "In all kinds of weather."

"Then I'm in good hands," he said.

She smiled modestly. "I don't mean to brag, I just didn't want you to worry."

"I'm not worried. I'm impressed. Where are we going exactly?" he asked. Since the engine blocked his view from the windshield, he turned to look out the side window.

"Mystic is fifty miles from here," she said. "Due northwest. It's not much. Just a dot on the map. But it's home. I've lived there most of my life, except for when I went away to school.''

His brain was buzzing with questions. Who do you live with, how did you happen to be here, why did you come to Alaska in the first place and what do you do there? And most of all, are you married? Why did he care? After today, he'd never see her again. But he did care. He glanced casually at her left hand on the throttle. No ring. That didn't mean a thing. He'd learned a few things from the lectures on board the cruise ship. The bush was a rough and wild place. Not as rough as it was during the Gold Rush, where the men carried pick axes and the women followed them to the gold camps where they became dance-hall girls and prostitutes, but it was still not a place for weaklings. He suspected Carrie Porter was not a weakling. He also suspected not many women lived alone in the Alaska bush. If they did, they didn't look like her.

He couldn't help it. He had to know. ''You live alone?'' he asked casually.

''Now I do,'' she said without looking at him. She stared straight ahead, her chin at a stubborn angle, her profile outlined against the gray sky outside her window. ''Ever since my dad died over a year ago.''

He nodded sympathetically. He didn't know how much longer his own father would be around, but he knew what a gap his death would leave in his life.

''It must be lonely,'' he said.

''You're wrong,'' she said with a flash of irritation, as if she'd been told that before. ''I like living alone. It's not lonely at all. Mystic is known as the friend-liest village in Alaska. For good reason. People there take care of each other. Even if you're only there for an hour, you'll see.''

He shot her a curious glance and wondered if she didn't protest a little too much about not being lonely.

''I'll take your word for it,'' he assured her.

''We're coming up on the eagle nests,'' she said, abruptly changing the subject. ''I'll bank to the right so you can look down on the cliffs. November and December are the best months for viewing, but there should be a few early birds around looking for salmon in the river. They make their nests in little crevices in the rocks.''

''Yes, I think I just saw one. There's another. Amazing,'' he said. He took his camera out of his bag and leaned against the window to snap picture after picture. ''This is beautiful country,'' he said, taking in the snow-capped mountains in the distance and the rushing river below. ''It's like nothing I've ever seen before. I can't believe I'm still in America.''

Carrie smiled to herself. She'd heard it all before. The gasps, the exclamations. For the wonder at the size of the fiftieth state, the wilderness and the stunning scenery. But this time it meant more. For some reason it was very important to her that this man appreciate her home state.

''I know,'' she said. ''I've flown over it hundreds of times, from Nome to Barrow to Juneau with freight and people and it still blows me away. I never get over it.''

''This is your job then?''

''What I'm doing today? Not really. Mostly I haul freight.'' She nodded her head toward the space behind the seats. "I've occasionally med-evaced people out before, in an emergency, but I'm not really set up for it. I don't have the space for a gurney or anything. Besides, I was afraid to move Donny."

"You did the right thing," he said.

"I hope so. I just hope I'm not too late. If I hadn't connected with you, I would have had to go farther, spent more time looking. I'm so grateful to you."

"You say there's no nurse in town? Not even a paramedic?"

"Mystic isn't exactly a booming metropolis. Since the gold rush of 1898 the population has been dwindling."

"Then why…"

"Why do I stay? It's my home." She couldn't help the edge that crept into her voice. She was tired of explaining to school friends and relatives in the lower forty-eight why she stayed after her father died. Maybe because she didn't have a good answer. Maybe because she would never admit there were times when she was unbearably lonely or that the life her father had made for them wasn't good enough for her. If she left, it would be a repudiation of everything he stood for—independence, loyalty, persistence.

"I was going to ask why your father came. Surely not for gold."

"He was a navy pilot. After the Korean war he came up here and flew for one of the small airlines. He found a piece of land on the peninsula near Mystic, with water on three sides, solitude and all the salmon he could eat. He thought he'd died and gone to heaven. He bought a plane, this plane, and went into business for himself. Typical Alaskan, he never did like taking orders from anyone.''

''So it all worked out,'' Matt said. ''He got what he wanted.''

''All that and heaven, too. Except for my mother. He didn't get her. An isolated ghost town a thousand miles from civilization was not her idea of heaven. She went back to California.''

''She didn't take you with her?''

''I wouldn't go. I've always had a stubborn streak. Typical Alaskan,'' she said with a rueful smile. ''Besides…'' Never mind. No need to go into details with a stranger. Fortunately they were nearing the Mystic peninsula and she didn't have time to think about the day her mother left. She was proud of the way she'd handled his question, the way she'd handled the many questions about her upbringing, especially about her mother. Carrie had it down pat. They'd given her the choice to stay or go. She'd made her choice and she was sticking by it. She could leave anytime, but she wouldn't. It was time to stop talking about herself. She'd said entirely too much already.

Carrie found it was usually easier to duck questions about her personal life and her history. Everybody in Mystic either already knew the answers or knew better than to ask. But this man had an uncanny way of drawing her out. Before she knew it she was blabbing about her mother and her father and herself as if they were the most interesting people in the world.

''Fascinating,'' Matt said. She felt his gaze resting on her.

''Not really,'' she said. ''The truth is everyone in Alaska has a story to tell. How they got here, why they stayed and so forth. It's a colorful land, filled with colorful people. You'll see.'' She glanced out her side window. ''Here we are. Mystic is just ahead of us. Can you see that fjord down there? The town is on the spit of land. Thank God the weather's holding. I thought maybe…''

Why burden the doctor needlessly with fears of fog or wind and rain. She just prayed she could get him back as promised. Even better, she prayed he would be able to help Donny. Because if he couldn't…she didn't know what she'd do. She bit her lip and turned on the radio. Static filled the cabin. She picked up the microphone.

''Joe, can you hear me? It's Carrie. I'm almost home. About ten minutes away.''

''Carrie. Glad you got back. I heard on the TV there's a big front coming down from the Aleutians.''

''Really?'' She felt a shimmy of fear go up her spine. ''I don't see anything from up here. What's it like down there?''

''The wind picked up about an hour ago. You better come down quick.''

''Okay. I'm bringing a doctor for Donny.''

''That's good news. I'll call over there and tell them.''

''If the wind's as strong as you say, I'm going to land out a ways and taxi in to my dock. As soon as I tie up, I'll head for town.''

She glanced at Matt. ''Don't worry. I've landed in much rougher weather than this.''

He nodded and smiled calmly at her as if they'd been flying together for years instead of only minutes. How did he know she'd bring him in safely? Maybe it was the same way she knew he was a good doctor. Intuition.

She appreciated his confidence, but maybe he should be concerned, because if Joe was right and the weather got any worse, he wasn't going to make it back to the ship tonight. Would he still be smiling when he was stuck in Mystic, a one-horse town with no amenities to speak of? She knew what strangers thought of it and how eager they were to leave even after a short visit.

As she lowered her altitude she flew through layers of rain and wind and fog. So the front was already there. In spite of it, she made a decent landing, one her father would have been proud of. She could hear his voice now, "Keep your eye on the instruments, Carrie. Your life depends on them." There were times when her intuition told her one thing and the instruments would tell her another. It was so easy to be fooled when flying at night or through gray skies. She'd only been fooled once, and that had nothing to do with flying. Taxiing in across the water was rough. Salt spray covered the windows whenever the little plane pitched forward as it skimmed the water and headed toward land.

Automatically, she reached and put her hand on Matt's arm. "We're almost there," she said. "Sorry about this rough weather. It gets bumpy from time to time. It can be scary if you're not used to it. But I've done this many times, so just relax."

He grinned. "Relax? Are you kidding? This is better than a roller coaster. I'm having the time of my life."

She gave him a quick smile in return, then concentrated on bringing the plane in. Through the spray on the windshield she saw a small group of people on her dock. Joe must have spread the word. As she touched the dock, Matt unfastened his seat belt and opened the door to leap from the plane to the dock over a large gap of churning water. Without her saying a word of instruction he threw a rope around a post just as she'd done in Tongass. It was so much easier with two. The thought that *life* was much easier with two flitted through her mind. This was not the time to dwell on that. Not with a crowd waiting for her and a medical emergency to deal with.

When she cut the engine, Matt held out his hand to help her out. He had a firm grip that didn't let her go until she had both feet firmly on the ground. His hand was strong and warm in hers. It was a surgeon's hand, she thought as she turned to the worried faces of Donny's father, his aunt and uncle and several other villagers.

"Carrie," his father shouted as tears ran down his face. "Thank God you're back. Come quick. Come now. It's Donny. He's dying."

She staggered backward. No, it couldn't be. She'd failed. She hadn't been fast enough. Matt caught her around the waist and held her tightly. He held out his other hand and introduced himself to Donny's father. He stood in the wind and the rain and exuded confidence. She heard him tell Donny's father he'd do everything he could. And she saw the grateful look on the father's face as he clasped the doctor's hand between his.

Chapter Two

Carrie took a deep breath. Though she was trembling on the inside, she managed to get control of herself. She realized that Donny's father was nearly hysterical and, as such, might not be the best judge of his son's condition. He was clearly distraught and grateful at the same time. He told Matt he was afraid even if Donny lived he'd never walk again. He said his son was in pain, he couldn't breathe, couldn't move.

Carrie ran to back her truck out of the garage. The others took off and Matt got into her truck. It was just a short ride to town and Donny's house. She was hoping against hope it wasn't true. He couldn't be dying. Not yet. Not when she'd brought a doctor to save him.

Carrie felt frozen, inside and out. She turned the heat up to high in the truck but still she shivered uncontrollably. All day long her only thought had been of bringing someone to save the boy. Against all odds she'd done it, and now she feared she was too late. She couldn't speak. She'd run out of words and out of energy. She'd used up her reserves. She was too late. Too late. The words repeated over and over in her mind, matching the rhythm of the windshield wipers.

Matt put his hand on her shoulder. She was glad for the distraction. Glad for his company. "The father is understandably worried," he said. "On the verge of hysteria, which can be contagious, if you let it. I did what I could to reassure him. You know you've done everything you could. Now let me take over. But don't fall apart on me. I might need your help."

She turned to face him. He was so calm, so incredibly unruffled even after a flight to the edge of the world, a bumpy landing and a case he wasn't prepared to take on. The warmth from his hand spread to the cold, empty space beneath her ribs. She took a shaky breath and nodded.

"Sorry. I don't know what happened to me. I'll be fine."

"Good girl. While you were getting the truck I told the father I'd do what I could. Make a diagnosis, confer with my experts by phone, start treatment, everything that's humanly possible."

Carrie felt herself warming up at last. From her toes to her head. It was partly the heater and it was also his soothing words that gave her confidence that everything was going to be all right. Or maybe it was the fact that she had someone to share her concern with. It had been a long time. When her father was here things were different. Theirs was a relationship based on respect and admiration and, of course, love. Growing up, he'd been her mother and father both. She missed him badly. When he died, friends asked what she was going to do. She'd answered automatically: "Stay right here, of course. Take over the business."

But sometimes in the middle of the night, when the wolves howled in the distance and the brown bears knocked over the garbage can, or when she flew into the sunrise by herself, leaving an empty house on a cold, dark morning, she wondered if she was doing the right thing, staying on by herself.

Down a dirt road, past the post office and the store, in the doorway of a small prefabricated house, Donny's mother, Tillie, waited in the doorway, her broad face creased with worry lines.

"Thank God you've come," she told Carrie.

"I've brought the doctor," Carrie said. The woman nodded gratefully, her eyes on the tall man with the black bag under his arm. She led Matt to the kitchen so he could wash up.

Carrie stayed in the living room with five or ten friends, Donny's younger sisters and brothers, and some aunts and uncles, while Matt went into the boy's bedroom. She wanted to go in the bedroom to see for herself what Donny's condition really was, but she sensed they didn't need any more bodies than the immediate family in there, any other voices to add to the confusion. The group in the living room spoke in hushed voices. Carrie quietly told the story of how she'd found Matt and what a lucky chance it was.

When Matt finally came out of the bedroom with Donny's parents, he told everyone he'd given Donny some pain medicine and a shot of cortisone to reduce the swelling along his spinal cord. He was already much more comfortable. He said that he didn't know for sure without an X ray or a CAT scan, but in his opinion, the accident had caused a compression injury to Donny's spinal cord. By stabilizing his condition, he ought to get well enough to travel and get treatment at the nearest hospital. But not for a while.

"It's important for him to get bed rest. If he regains movement in his lower body within a week that will mean that he'll probably recover completely in time with treatment and rehabilitation. But I don't know anything for sure. If I had an X-ray machine, I'd have a better idea. All I can tell you is he'll need lots of attention as well as your love and your prayers."

They looked somewhat relieved. They nodded and they all talked at once. Everyone had a question.

"Will he get well?"

"Will he ever walk again?"

"When can he be moved?"

"How long can you stay?"

Matt answered them all as patiently and diplomatically as he could. But Carrie thought he must be anxious to leave. She glanced out the window. In the excitement she'd forgotten her concern with the weather. She hadn't even noticed the rain pelting the glass and the wind whistling around the house. Oh, Lord, what if she couldn't take off? What if she couldn't get Matt back as she'd promised? After all he'd done for her and for Donny and for his family.

Though worried about the weather, she felt such a huge surge of relief to hear Matt's diagnosis. She hoped he wasn't giving them false hopes. She too had more questions, but she'd wait her turn. She sat on the arm of a padded chair and let her muscles relax and the tension ooze out of her body for the first time since she'd started out that morning. She didn't realize until that moment how very tired she was. The muscles in her legs ached, and she longed to sink down into the chair and close her eyes. But that wouldn't do. She had to be the pillar of strength everyone expected.

After more questions and more expressions of gratitude and tea that Tillie made and served to the whole group, Carrie asked Matt if she could see Donny.

After Matt had a brief word with his parents, Carrie tiptoed into the small bedroom with the posters of rock stars on the walls. The boy's eyes were closed. His face was almost as white as the sheet tucked around him. His head was propped on two pillows and he looked terribly uncomfortable. She blinked back a tear.

"Hi, sport," she said softly. "I hope you get better soon."

His eyelids fluttered. Maybe he heard her. Maybe he didn't. She turned and left.

On the way to her truck, Carrie scanned the skies. As the wind whipped her hair across her face and the rain drenched her jacket, she knew what she'd feared was true. She couldn't fly in this weather. She and Matt drove slowly down the dirt road to her house, as the rain filled the potholes and beat against the windshield. She had to tell him that he wasn't going back to the ship today. She pulled into the garage and sat there. Instead of saying what she had to say, she first had to ask him a question.

"Is it true what you said?" she asked. "You really think it's possible he's going to be all right? Or was that just wishful thinking?"

"Doctors don't deal in wishful thinking," he said

with a frown, turning to face her. "At least I don't. Patients deserve to hear the truth. Most people can deal with it. From what I observed, I think it's possible he could have a good chance for a complete recovery. Or he could be paralyzed from the hips down for the rest of his life. It's just hard to say without a workup in a hospital. I hope I didn't convey the impression that everything was okay and that complete recovery is guaranteed. I couldn't possibly know that. The best thing to do is get him to a hospital after his swelling has gone down, he'll get a workup and a diagnosis and the proper treatment, whatever it is."

"I'll do it. I'll have him med-evaced or take him to Anchorage myself if I have to. But why did they tell us he was dying?"

"He didn't look good when we got there. He was in pain and he thought he was going to die. Sudden disability in an active young person is almost always followed by shock and acute depression. But he's got some reflex action. Not much, but some. There are other encouraging signs. Enough signs to be hopeful, cautiously hopeful. He's lucky he didn't land on his head."

"How will we know when it's all right to move him?"

"I told his parents and I'll tell you what signs to look for. As I said, we'll know a lot more in one week."

She nodded. "I'm so relieved. I was terribly worried. I had no idea what was going to happen. I've known Donny all his life. Well, I've known most of the kids in town for that long. But he's special, he's the oldest of eight kids and the brightest. We talk about books and he asks me questions about the world outside. I hope he'll get a chance to see it for himself. He should go to college, though most of the kids here don't. I'd like to see to it he has an opportunity to go on."

"Like you did."

"Yes."

"But you came back."

"That was my choice. He might make a different one. The point is I had a choice. Most of the young people here don't. They don't have the money or the drive to go anywhere."

"Tell me, Carrie," he said, running his hand through his damp hair. Her startled gaze collided briefly with his. He'd never called her by her name before. She'd never called him by his. She knew what he was going to say. *Tell me, Carrie, when can I get out of this godforsaken town?* She knew because she'd heard it before.

But he didn't. He seemed to forget what he was going to say. He sat there for a good long minute while he looked at her. The tension built. She knotted her fingers together in her lap. Their glances held and something passed between them. She didn't know what it was. She didn't know what it meant, but it left her wondering what was going to happen if she let it.

She was conscious of his lean, tall body, of the strength in his hands. Of his eyes and the way he looked at her as if he knew everything about her. How could he know that if he kissed her she would kiss him back, before she even knew it herself? How could he possibly know how much she needed someone like him. Someone strong and smart and capable and sexy. Oh yes, very sexy.

She knew he could save lives. She knew he was going to be a great doctor. Even more important, she knew he was a good man. There was only a small space between them. She knew how little it would take to bridge that space. He did, too. The windows fogged up and it was just the two of them inside a truck in a remote corner of the world. If she leaned toward him, just a fraction of an inch…if he leaned toward her…

But she didn't. Neither did he.

Finally he spoke and snapped the cord that stretched between them. "Tell me, Carrie, if this is the friendliest village in Alaska, why are we sitting in your truck instead of going inside your house?"

She almost laughed with relief. Relief tinged with disappointment. Nothing had happened between them. Nothing was going to happen. She had to tell him they weren't going to get out of this friendly town anytime soon, but maybe she could postpone it for a few more minutes. The least she could do was invite him in and give him something to eat and drink. And the most? She didn't want to consider that.

They took off their wet shoes and left them at the back door. He followed her into the kitchen. She handed him a towel, and he mopped the water from his face and took off his jacket. She hadn't realized how big he was, how much he would fill up her kitchen. He stood in the middle of the room, tall, broad-shouldered, not knowing how he looked almost at home there and what an effect that had on her. He wasn't looking at her, he was looking at the cast-iron cookstove and the table made from lumber from a fallen spruce. "This is an amazing house."

"My father built it with stone from the quarry," she said, lighting the paper under the kindling in the pot-bellied stove in the corner.

"But you decorated it," he said, looking around at the hand-stenciled cupboards and the tiled counters.

"Well, yes, such as it is. We're a little short on interior decorators up here, so it's pretty much do-it-yourself or don't do it at all."

Instead of standing there gaping in wonder at the unlikely sight of a handsome, big-city doctor in her kitchen, instead of planning how she was going to tell him he wasn't going anywhere else that day, she opened the draft on the stove and watched the small sticks of wood catch fire. Then she pulled a jar from the freezer and held it up.

"Do you like salmon?" she asked. "I can offer you some chowder I made."

"Sounds good," he said.

She put the frozen soup into a pot and stirred it vigorously over a low flame on the stovetop.

She set her spoon down, reached for a bottle of dark red claret and poured two glasses. Her hand brushed his when she handed one to him. She felt a brief zing like an electric current race through her body. Startled, she looked at him. What had happened? Did he feel anything? Apparently not from the bland expression on his face. He looked more interested in the wine than in her.

He rolled the wine around in the glass, then took an appreciative sip as if nothing had happened. It hadn't. Except in her imagination. "Don't tell me you made this, too?" he asked.

She shook her head. "I tried to make wine once out of berries, but it turned out more like vinegar. I try my best to be self-sufficient, but there are some things I just can't do. No, someone gave this to me. I gave him a ride in my boat to a nearby island. He gave me the wine in exchange. We do a lot of bartering up here."

He swirled the wine around in the glass and studied it thoughtfully. "Is there a man in your life, Carrie?"

She set her glass down with a thud.

"I'm sorry. I had no business asking," he said. "But it's not every day I meet a beautiful bush pilot with red hair and eyes the color of amber." He leaned forward, met her gaze and caught a strand of her hair to wind it around his finger. "Or are they more like caramel?"

She felt the heat rise to her head. Her face flamed. If she wasn't used to strange men in her kitchen who smelled like leather and expensive soap and wore designer khakis, she was even more unused to extravagant compliments from strange men.

"They're just hazel," she said, edging backward and forcing him to drop his hand. "You're not used to bush pilots and I'm not used to strangers in my kitchen. Or flattery. Everyone up here is pretty plainspoken and they accept me for what I am. They know all about me."

"Do they?" he said. "Do they know you blush when you get a compliment? That your hair is the color of a new penny?"

She blushed again. She cursed herself for acting

like an adolescent. She cursed herself for not being more worldly, for not having a snappy retort for every compliment. She cursed the weather for preventing her from taking him back to his ship today.

"Well, they know I live alone. And that I like it that way. That I once had a boyfriend, a long time ago. That it didn't work out and that's okay. That I've never applied for a job in my life. I inherited my job, my plane and this house. I think I'm lucky and I like my life the way it is."

"That's it? That's the whole story?" he asked.

She shrugged. "That's all there is. Sorry it's not more exciting."

"You make a living flying all over in your own floatplane. You grew up in a village with bears and totem poles and you think your life is not exciting? If it isn't then I don't know what is."

He looked at her as if she was some form of rare and exotic Alaskan wildlife. Maybe she was. Apparently he'd never met anyone like her before. She had to admit she felt the same about him. But then, she didn't get out of the sparsely populated state much, which suited her fine.

She ladled out some soup into two bowls and set them on the wooden table. Then she took a deep breath. "I'm not going to be able to fly you back tonight, Matt." She almost stumbled over his name. She wished she could call him Dr. Baker, it would help her keep in mind he was a doctor and out of her league, but at this point it would be ridiculous. "I'm sorry. I know I promised but…"

"Never mind," he said, pulling a chair up to the table. "It will give me a chance to check up on Donny tomorrow. You can take me to Skagway tomorrow. I'll meet the ship there. I'll get a room in a hotel or something tonight.''

"Or something is more like it,'' Carrie said, sitting down across from him. "I wish there was a hotel in Mystic, but there isn't. We don't get that many tourists. The nearest hotel is in Stewart, fifty miles as the crow or the floatplane flies. They've also got a coffeehouse. We're lucky to have a post office, a store, a school and a library, which is only open when I'm home because I'm the librarian. Oh, and a kind of museum, too.''

"Which is only open when you're home because you're probably the curator,'' he said, digging into his soup.

"How did you know?'' she asked.

"Just a lucky guess. I suppose you caught the salmon for the soup. It's great.''

"Actually I traded it for a pan of cinnamon rolls, I've never been much of a fisherman.''

"I don't know who got the best deal,'' Matt said. "I guess I'd have to taste those rolls first.'' He imagined how she'd look in her kitchen in the morning, any morning, with her hair tousled, her eyes still sleepy and the scent of yeast and cinnamon in the air, and it caused his heart to pump double time. What a combination—she was modest, gutsy, gorgeous, warm, generous and self-effacing. It was just his luck to find her in this corner of a different world. A world seen by most through the porthole of a cruise ship. It was his luck to see it up close and firsthand. If only he'd seen it ten years ago.

If only he'd met her then in a different place and

a different time. Things might have been…no, ten years ago he was on his way to becoming a doctor. He wouldn't have let anything interfere with his plans, or were they his father's plans? It didn't matter. The die had been cast. The end was almost in sight. Three more years. Now if only the boy would recover, he would always have happy memories of this place. He'd always keep her image in one corner of his mind.

"If that's a hint, you're on," Carrie said. "After all you've done for me, for us, for the town, I'll do whatever it takes to make your stay more pleasant. Cinnamon rolls, whatever."

"Anything?" he asked, trying to sound casual, but feeling anything but. He felt downright lecherous. He had no idea what was happening to him. If he thought about it, which he really didn't want to do, he'd have to say that it was being here, away from everything and everybody he knew that had him feeling like a different person from the focused, serious medical resident who'd left for a vacation with his parents a week ago. It was his first break in a long time, between med school and his internship.

Sometimes it seemed he'd spent all his life studying. Was he acting out because of the spring breaks from college that he'd never had, was he trying to make up for the teen summers spent in summer school while other guys chased bikini-clad girls on the beach? Had he missed out on something by staying away from womanizing and drinking binges in college?

Whatever it was, he had it bad. He tried not to stare at her, but it was hard not to. Even as he was eating

he let his gaze cross the table. When she wasn't looking, he studied her cheekbones, her eyes, the way her
hair fell across her cheek. He couldn't tear his eyes
away from her. His first break, his first crush, about
ten years too late. That's all it was, a crush on a
woman who was everything he wasn't. Free and easy.
And self-sufficient. So self-sufficient she didn't need
anybody. Except for the whole town. Or did they need
her more than she needed them?

There was something about her that made him
aware of every move she made. Whether it was her
hands on the controls or her head bent over the pot
of soup. Every gesture fascinated him, every word she
spoke intrigued him. For a moment there in the truck
he thought he might kiss her. She thought about it,
too. He knew she did. She wore her thoughts on her
face and her heart on her sleeve. But he'd caught
himself in time. He still wanted to kiss her. He wanted
to tangle his fingers in her red-gold hair. Just winding
a tendril around his finger had only made him want
more. Much more. He also wanted to know more
about her. He wanted to know everything.

Good thing he was leaving tomorrow. His life was
planned. The job, the career. Even the wife.

"I'd do *almost* anything," she said in answer to
his question. "I, uh, look Matt, you're welcome to
stay here tonight. In fact, you don't have a lot of
choices. It's the guest room or the couch," she said
firmly.

She might blush, she might stutter, she might be
uneasy, but she'd put him in his place. Whatever he
was feeling for her, she wanted no part of. But if it
was true, there was no man in her life, it was a

damned shame and a waste of a remarkable woman. Why, he wanted to ask. Why not?

"Fortunately some of my dad's clothes are still in boxes waiting to be given away. Jackets, sweaters, pants, even boots, something ought to fit you. Just in case…" She glanced out the window where, given the dusk and the fog, it was hard to see more than a few yards.

"Which reminds me," he said. "I have to call the ship and let my parents know I won't be back tonight. I also might call a surgeon I know in San Francisco, to get his advice about your friend Donny. And to make sure I'm doing the right thing."

"The phone's in the living room." She led the way to a wood paneled room with a huge leather couch, a large stone fireplace where a fire was laid, a fur rug in front of it and native blankets hanging on the walls. It looked like a ski lodge. The kind of place to curl up with a good book or a good woman. He watched Carrie bend over to light the fire, noticed the sweet curve of her hip in her jumpsuit, and a sharp stab of desire flooded his body.

Well, what harm did it do to fantasize about a woman he would never see again after tomorrow? What harm to fantasize about a different life, a simple life here in the Alaska bush, where men were men and women, at least one woman, looked like something off the cover of *Country Life* or *Aviation* magazine or maybe even *Vogue?* Where evenings like this were spent in simple and basic pursuits… He told himself not to go there, that the fantasy was getting out of hand.

Carrie fanned the flames of the fire and stood up.

She gave him a look as if she knew what he was thinking and those thoughts disturbed her. Could she possibly be thinking the same thing? Forget that. She'd brought him here for one reason and one reason alone. He had no right to hit on her.

She took a deep breath. "I'm going upstairs to shower and change," she said.

Matt nodded and watched her walk up the stairs. Her red hair bounced against her shoulders. Despite her fatigue, she exuded energy. He wished he could tap it and bottle it and sell it to his patients. Hell, what he really wanted was to keep it for himself.

He sat in a large leather recliner chair, called Information and got the number of an old family friend who was well established in neurosurgery in San Francisco. Luckily Jay was on call. He got him on his cell phone and was able to explain how the accident happened, list the boy's symptoms and the treatment he'd started. Jay assured Matt he had done all the right things. He made a few suggestions and also offered to look at the boy and do a workup if Matt could bring him down there.

"Sounds like you got there just in time with the steroids. Because if you hadn't and the nerves were totally destroyed...he could be totally paralyzed. If and when the boy can travel, I'd be glad to look at him and do the surgery myself, if that's what he needs."

"Thanks, Jay. He'd appreciate that. I'll get back to you."

"How long are you staying up there?"

"I don't know." Matt glanced out the window into the dark Alaskan night. "That depends on the weather. This is an isolated spot, accessible only by plane or boat. It doesn't look like I'll be flying out anytime soon.''

"Sounds like you got more than you bargained for on this trip.''

Jay could have no idea just how much Matt had gotten out of this trip. This was no time to go into details.

"Talk to you later,'' he said.

Then Matt fished a piece of paper from his pocket and tried to make sense of the numbers that would let him call the ship. He picked up the phone and punched in the number. There was no answer in his parents' cabin. The ship's operator could only promise to deliver the message. He hung up somewhat relieved. He really didn't want to hear his father remind him how important this vacation was, maybe their last together, or hear his mother sound wistful about his absence.

"Did you reach them?'' Carrie asked, fifteen minutes later. She was in stocking feet, wearing black stretch pants that hugged her hips and her long legs like a second skin, and a pink sweater that drew his attention to the outline of her breasts. It was quite a change from the unisex jumpsuit she'd been wearing. Her hair was damp and curled around her face. The light scent of flowery soap wafted his way. He sucked in a deep breath. He had a feeling it was going to be a long night. A long frustrating night.

"I got ahold of my friend the surgeon. He had a few suggestions, and he even offered to treat Donny, if you can get him down to San Francisco. He's an expert in spinal-cord injuries and the best person you could get. But he won't be able to help until Donny's condition is stabilized.''

''That's wonderful. I wouldn't have known where to turn for the best treatment. I just hope…'' She nodded as if to reassure herself as well as him. ''We'll get him there somehow.''

''I called the ship and left a message. I also left your number. I hope you don't mind.''

''I hope they won't worry,'' she said, one hand on the back of a chair.

''I'm afraid it's built in. Parents always worry. At least mine do. Don't tell me your father didn't worry when you were out flying.''

''I'm sure he did. But he never said anything. Except to remind me a hundred times to watch out for crosswinds. They can come up here when you least expect them.''

''I'm almost glad I didn't have to talk to my parents,'' Matt said. ''My father will feel bad that he didn't insist on coming along. I think he might even be envious. Doctors spend so much time doing what they've been trained to do in a tightly controlled environment, this would have been something to tell his patients about. Of course he's enjoying the cruise, but coming here…'' He looked around her cabin as if he'd been transported to a rare and wonderful land. ''It's something special. On the ship tonight is the captain's champagne reception. It's a black-tie affair. That's where they'll be.''

''I can't offer you champagne or a black tie. But there's enough hot water left if you want a shower, and you can take your pick of the clothes in the bedroom on the left.''

''Thanks,'' he said, and went up the stairs.

Carrie put another log on the fire and watched the flames rise. It was only fall, but the radiant heat was welcome on a night like this. Even more welcome when the temperatures dropped below freezing in the winter. She sat on the stone hearth to let the heat dry her hair and thought about the man upstairs. What would her father say if he knew she'd invited a stranger to spend the night? The man who right now was standing under the shower with the water pouring down on his broad shoulders, who was soaping his chest while the lather cascaded down his legs....

Carrie took a deep breath and tried to think of something else. She couldn't. It wasn't her fault. She'd been alone too long. Too long since there'd been a man in her life.

'''Bout time,'' she imagined her father saying. ''Alaska is no place for a woman alone.'' She'd accuse him of being a chauvinist and he'd admit it. He wanted her to get married, but not to the man she'd brought home to meet him. As it turned out, he hadn't needed to worry.

The man she'd brought home today wasn't any more suitable than the first one. Surely her father would have seen that. It was obvious. She ought to find herself a fisherman, a logger or a hunter. Someone at home in the bush. Someone content to stay there. Because she had no intention of ever leaving God's country. She told herself to relax. No one was asking her to leave. Least of all a doctor who'd come to help out in an emergency. Maybe he found her interesting. Maybe he really thought she was beautiful. It wouldn't last. Although she was probably different from the women he knew, she was probably a little too different.

When he came down the stairs he was wearing her father's plaid flannel shirt and a pair of outdoor fishing pants with cargo pockets that were baggy but almost fitted him. Her father had been a large man. For a moment it seemed her father had come back. As if she weren't alone anymore. A tear sprang to her eye.

"Carrie? What is it?"

"It's the clothes. I'm sorry. I'm fine, really."

"I'll go back and change," he said turning toward the stairs.

She stood and crossed the room, put her hand on his arm. "No, don't. He'd want you to wear them. He'd want someone to get some use out of them. That's why I gave most of them away. He hated waste."

Matt brushed the tear from her cheek with the pad of his thumb. "Are you sure?" he asked.

She nodded. His touch was so tender, so unexpected, it set off a new round of tears. Instead of stopping, she cried harder. She'd received sympathy when her father died, but not this kind of comfort.

"What's wrong?" Matt asked, alarmed, both hands on her shoulders, holding her tight.

"I...I don't know. I didn't cry that much when he died. He didn't want me to. He was tough and he wanted me to be, too. I tried to be, but look at me now. I'm having a delayed reaction." She drew in a ragged breath. "I'm a mess."

"Go ahead and cry," he said. "Nobody can be tough all the time. Everybody has to let go after a tragedy. It's only normal. Sometimes it happens sooner, sometimes later.''

"You're not a psychiatrist, are you?'' she said between sniffles.

"No, I'm destined for plastic surgery. But I did a rotation in psychiatry once. It was fascinating and I learned a lot.''

Carrie wondered if it was there he learned how to comfort teary females or did it just come naturally. However it had happened he was an expert. He exuded strength, sympathy and understanding. And so much more.

"You've had a stressful day, flying around looking for a doctor,'' he said. "You flew us through rough weather and you had a scare about the boy.''

He put his arms around her and held her tight. It felt so good to be held, to have someone care about her. To admit to herself she was not as strong as she pretended. She had no idea why a stranger should be able to see into her mind the way no one else could. Maybe it was because she'd let down her guard for once. Maybe it was knowing she didn't have to put up a front for him. After all, she'd never see him again after tomorrow or the day after at the most.

She looped her arms around his neck and pressed her wet cheek against his shoulder. He was so warm, so big, so solid. He smelled like the rain and the wind and the shampoo in her bathroom and a deep, dark, masculine smell that was all his. Her tears dried but she didn't let go. Neither did he.

He cupped her face in his hands and looked deep into her eyes. "I've never known anyone like you.''

His voice dropped to a hoarse whisper. "Never seen anyone as beautiful."

Now was the time to be tough. She knew that. Now was the time to say thanks but no thanks, to smile and let go. Go make coffee. Go roll out the dough for the cinnamon buns. Anything but stand there and wait for him to kiss her. Because she knew he was going to. She could see it in his eyes. Hear it in his voice. Feel the vibrations in the air.

But when it came, she wasn't prepared. She wasn't prepared for his mouth to take possession of hers, for the passion behind it, or for the way she reacted. As if she'd never been kissed before. She hadn't. Not like that. His mouth was hard and hungry. As if making up for years of abstinence. As if he'd been waiting for her all his life.

She kissed him back. Softly at first then harder and faster as if she didn't have enough time. Deep down somewhere in the back of her mind she knew she was going to regret this. Maybe not tonight. Maybe not tomorrow. But soon and for a long time. Her knees were so weak she was afraid she would fall if he didn't hold her.

He pulled back just slightly. She was afraid he'd leave her there, deprived of his heat, his hard body against hers. But he didn't. He trailed hot kisses from her lips to her ear and back. She moaned, and he invaded her mouth with his tongue. She met him thrust for thrust and she still wanted more. She wanted all of him.

His hands slid under her sweater. Impatient, she struggled to take it off. She wanted nothing between them. Nothing.

That was when she heard the knock on the door. Dimly, as if it belonged to another house, another time. She wished it did. But it was her house and it was now.

She didn't know how she got to the door to open it, but she must have, because Stan, a local logger who'd had a crush on her for years was standing there, smiling shyly.

"Sorry to bother you, Carrie. But I heard you had a doctor here." His curious gaze traveled over her wrinkled sweater and her flushed cheeks.

"Oh…yes." She ran her hands through her hair. Yanked at the hem of her sweater. "Hi, Stan. Come on in. This is…this is…Dr. Baker."

Matt looked as if he was not at all surprised to have a patient come knocking on the door in a remote Alaskan village. He didn't seem to realize that his hair was a mess and the shirt he was wearing was tearstained. He was also breathing hard.

"Didn't mean to interrupt anything," Stan said, his eyes moving from Carrie to Matt and back again. "But I've been having this problem with my eye."

"Uh…Stan, Matt, Dr. Baker I mean, is just here on vacation… I mean he isn't…"

"Come on in. Let's have a look at it," Matt said, overriding her, just as if he was the resident physician, on call and ready for patients. Although it was past nine o'clock and this was strictly above and beyond the call of duty.

While she watched, Matt took charge. Leading Stan to the desk in the corner, he examined his eye under the gooseneck lamp. Then he asked Carrie to get the bag he'd brought from the ship. He asked Stan how long his eye had been swollen and red, told him he had a case of conjunctivitis and after digging through the bag, he found the appropriate eye drops the ship's doctor had provided just in case he needed them. He gave them to Stan with instructions to use them twice a day along with some antibiotic pills.

"You ought to be feeling better in a few days," Matt said.

"What if I don't?" Stan asked, standing in the doorway, pulling on his dark beard.

Matt reached into the black bag for a pad of paper. On it he wrote his name and phone number. "You can call me," he said. "I won't be back this way, but maybe I can help you, anyway."

"Thanks, Doc," he said. "How much do I owe you?"

"It's on the house," Matt said with a smile.

Stan thanked him again, but instead of leaving, he hesitated, glancing shyly at Carrie. "I've got the pine boards for that bookcase I'm making for you," he said. "You should come by and tell me how wide you want the shelves."

"I will. Thanks, Stan. I'd almost forgotten about it."

"I didn't," he said. "I remember the day you came by and we talked about my building it for you. You were wearing jeans and a yellow sweater. All this time I've been looking for just the right wood. Old growth, not too many knots…you know."

"I appreciate that. Matt, Stan is not just a logger, but also the best carpenter in the whole area. I'll drop by your shop just as soon as I can."

Stan nodded and closed the door behind him, his medicine clutched in his hand.

"Friend of yours?" Matt asked.

"Everyone in town is a friend of mine," she said.

"Everyone as fond of you as he is?" he asked.

"Let's just say there aren't many young unmarried people around, so we've been thrown together by people who naturally think we ought to be a couple, but..."

"He probably wouldn't object."

"He's a sweet guy. That was very nice of you to take care of him," Carrie said, turning off the desk light. She'd done everything she could to discourage Stan's attentions, but it was hard to avoid him in such a small town. And hard to avoid the gossip that was better than hard currency in their little pocket of civilization.

"How could I say no?" Matt asked. "I certainly don't mind at all. It reminds me of a rotation I did in general practice in a rural area of northern California. We saw everything and anything. I got to know the patients and their families. I almost wished... But by then I had my sights set on plastic surgery. It's a tradition in the family. My grandfather, my father and now me. Like you and flying. You're taking over the family business. So am I."

"Did you have a choice?" she asked, sitting on the couch.

He sat next to her and put his arm around her shoulders. It felt so right, so natural, she leaned back against his arm and sighed with contentment. How easy it would be to forget that tomorrow or the next day he'd most certainly be gone. He would leave her with a piece of paper with his name and number on it just like he gave Stan. And he'd tell her she could call him if she needed advice, but that it wasn't likely he'd be back this way. As if she didn't know.

"A choice? Of course. But my father's health isn't good. He's had two heart attacks. Now more than ever he's counting on me to take over his practice for him. Not today or tomorrow. I need more training, a long internship. But after that—" Matt cut himself off, suddenly depressed at the years ahead of sleepless nights, of being on call, endless rounds and memorizing details. Yet he was ready to be a doctor. He wanted to treat patients.

"Plastic surgery? Isn't that doing face-lifts and tummy tucks?" Carrie asked.

"Some plastic surgeons do that," he said. "I don't find that kind of work interesting. I intend to do reconstruction, like for example, cleft palates. But enough about the future," he said. "I don't want to think about it now. I still have so much work ahead of me it gets to be daunting. It's the present I'm interested in."

Matt sifted his hands through her hair and buried his face in her auburn curls. He wanted to bury himself in her body. He shocked himself at the strength of his feelings. He didn't expect the jolt of sexual desire that hit him like a bolt of lightning. He'd never wanted anybody the way he wanted her. But he wasn't into one-night stands, and neither was she. He might not know much about her, but he knew that.

"You smell so damned good," he said, his voice suddenly rocky and uneven. "And you feel so good."

She pulled away and stood up. "Why don't I make

some coffee?'' she said, her voice no steadier than his. She felt it, too. She had to. All this passion couldn't be one-sided.

"In other words," he said. "Back off, Matt."

"Yes," she said. "No. I don't know. I don't know what's happening to me." She avoided his gaze by staring at her stockinged feet.

"The same thing that's happening to me," he said, looking up at her. He couldn't stop staring at her scarlet cheeks, her rumpled clothes and her tousled hair. He wanted more than anything to carry her up those stairs to her bedroom, the one he'd seen after his shower. The one with the braided rug on the floor and the down comforter on the queen-size bed. "I'd call it delayed adolescence, or spontaneous combustion or just plain lust. But I don't know. I only know it's never happened to me before."

She looked up. The firelight picked up green flecks in her soft eyes and they glowed in the firelight. "Me, neither," she said softly. "I just don't know what to do about it, except make coffee."

"I have a few ideas," he said. "We could start where we left off before that knock on the door."

He watched her closely. She seemed to be wavering. Make coffee or make love. No, he couldn't. He couldn't make love to her tonight and walk out tomorrow. Call it honor or call it self-preservation, he couldn't do it. But he wanted to. He wanted to so badly he ached.

"Make coffee," he said, forcing himself to sound normal, as if his heart wasn't banging against his chest. "We'll talk. I want to hear the story of your life."

"You've heard it," she said. "Plain coffee or Irish?"

"Whatever you're having."

She nodded and left the room. He paced back and forth in her father's sealskin moccasins in front of the windows, listening to the wind howling outside, hearing the rain slant huge drops against the windows. Inside it was warm and snug, thanks to her father, who'd built this house, and thanks to her for stockpiling firewood and food to keep them both warm and dry and well fed in the middle of the bush in an Alaskan storm. At the same time he was strung out like a taut wire. He wanted to follow her into the kitchen. He wanted to watch her make coffee. He wanted to memorize her every move, her every gesture. But he didn't. Instead he forced himself to sit down again and take a deep breath and calm down.

Chapter Three

Matt stretched his legs out in front of him and watched the flames in the stone fireplace. He tried not to think of what he was missing by backing off. He tried not to worry about how he was going to be able to sleep while under the same roof as her.

She came back a while later with two cups of coffee and a plate of warm cookies that smelled like spices. She deliberately sat opposite him in a large, overstuffed chair with the coffee table between them.

He picked up his coffee cup and held it to his lips. She had laced it with cream and Irish whiskey. It went down his throat as smooth as honey. Warming and filling him with contentment as it went. He leaned back and smiled at her. ''I have a feeling I only got the condensed version of your life story. I think you left out a few details,'' he said.

''Maybe. I didn't tell you about the day a bear came out of the woods when I was in the hot springs.''

''Hot springs, here?''

''On an island just a short hop away. I flew with some friends in the middle of winter. They were fishing, I was soaking in the springs. A brown bear came out of the woods and scared me half to death. I was afraid to get out.''

The image of Carrie naked in the bubbling springs, the steam rising, her body turning pink, her hair tumbling on her bare shoulders was almost too much for him to take. He had a hard time following the rest of the story.

''What happened?'' he asked. ''Did you escape or did you get eaten alive?''

''I knew you weren't listening,'' she said. ''You're somewhere else.''

''I'm at the hot springs,'' he confessed. ''Or I wish I were.''

''If we had time, I'd take you in my boat,'' she said. ''It's a beautiful spot.''

He thought about the cruise ship, with its gambling casino, dance floor and nightclub entertainment and a spa next to the pool on the main deck. That was where he'd be tomorrow. He could soak in hot water there with his parents and Mira. Not in a natural hot spring on an isolated island with Carrie. He forced himself to remember his obligations.

''You have a boat, too?'' he asked.

''A small launch. I ferry people to other islands sometimes. When the planes are grounded, it's the only way to get around.''

''Some other time,'' he said, ''I'd like to go.''

''Sure.'' But they both knew there wouldn't be any other time. ''I should check the weather,'' she said. She opened a cabinet to reveal a small TV set. ''We have a satellite dish out back. We ought to be able to get something.''

They got something. They got the Anchorage station. He watched the weather woman point to clouds, talk about rain and fog and speculate about wind conditions. He found it hard to concentrate.

"I hate to say this, but you may not get out tomorrow," she said with a frown.

"I hate to say this, but I don't really give a damn," he said, draining his cup.

"That may be the Irish whiskey talking," she said. "You may feel different tomorrow."

Before he could say anything the phone rang. They sat there listening to it. Each reluctant to have the evening interrupted by someone from the outside.

"It might be another patient. Word must be getting around," she said.

"I don't mind. I'll see anybody who needs me. Answer it."

But it wasn't a patient. Wordlessly, Carrie handed him the phone. It was Mira. He instantly regretted leaving his number with his parents. But what if there'd been an emergency? What if his father had another heart attack? If he had, there was still nothing he could do, he reminded himself. He was stuck in Mystic. For better or worse. At the moment it was not only better. It was the best.

"That's right," he said to Mira. "I'm stuck here for the night. Sorry I missed the party but I guess you heard there was a medical emergency. I'll catch up with you tomorrow in Skagway if the weather clears."

Mira expressed alarm that he might not get back the next day. He tried to reassure her, telling her he was fine, seeing a few patients besides the boy he'd come to see. She described the reception, the trip to the bald eagle reserve, and all the while he was watching Carrie, watching her clear the cups and take the tray to the kitchen. Without her in the room he should be able to pay attention to what Mira was saying, but he couldn't. He did hear her ask who that woman was who answered the phone.

"That was the bush pilot who flew me here," he said. "The one who will take me back tomorrow."

"Are you staying at a hotel?"

"There are no hotels. She was good enough to put me up for the night."

"Oh."

Mira wouldn't say anything else. But he could tell she was worried. In all the years he'd known her, she'd never had any competition. Except for his career. Now that he was almost in a position to find a wife, and she'd waited patiently for him to propose, this was no time for someone to pop up out of nowhere.

She talked a little more about the ship's activities, about the menu at dinner and the plans for the next day, while he could hear Carrie working in the kitchen. Finally he hung up. He found Carrie kneading dough on a large butcher block in the middle of the kitchen.

"That was Mira," he said. "She's on the cruise with her parents who are best friends of my parents. I don't know why she called."

Carrie looked up. There was a smudge of flour on her cheek. "Maybe she misses you."

He shrugged. "Anyone who gets involved with a doctor better get used to missing them."

"Is she involved with you?" She pushed a stray lock of hair behind her ear, leaving a trail of flour mixed with the copper strands of hair.

"Never mind. Don't answer that. It's none of my business. I shouldn't have asked."

"You can ask anything you want," he said. "The answer is I don't know. Our parents have been pushing us together since we were children. Given the commitment to med school, I've been too busy to look around. Mira hasn't found anyone else, either, so everyone has taken that to mean that Mira and I will end up together. This cruise was supposed to bring about a decision. At last."

"Has it?"

"No. I thought at one point it would make sense to marry Mira. But making sense is not something at the top of my list of things to do."

"What is?"

"You really want to know?" he asked, bracing his hands on the other side of the butcher block and fixing his steady gaze on her. "I want to make love to you on that fur rug in front of the fireplace in there. I thought about carrying you up the stairs, but right now I don't think I can make it. Besides I want to see your skin by firelight. I want to see the flames reflected in your eyes. I want to see your hair on your naked shoulders and…"

"Stop," she said with a gasp.

He stopped.

He waited for her to say something. He couldn't tell what she thought. The brightness in her eyes was either tears of joy or dismay. She might throw him out in the rain or start for the living room to turn down the lights and tear off her clothes. He hoped for the latter.

"This is pretty ridiculous," she said at last, transferring the dough from one hand to the other. "You just met me. You've known this Mira for years. I don't know what's happening here, but it doesn't take an analyst to make an educated guess. You've been studying and working for years without any breaks. All of a sudden you get a break you never expected. You're transported to a different world where you know no one. None of the old rules seem to apply. As for me, I've been alone, isolated, except for a whole town that appreciates me, and I don't have anyone special. You come along and..."

"And what?" he asked. He wanted her to say it. He wanted her to say that she wanted him as much as he wanted her. That she wanted to make love all night under a slanted roof or in front of a fire on a fur rug.

"And I completely lose it. I cry, I cling, I see things that aren't there, I imagine things that aren't going to happen. I'm a strong, independent woman. I have a life. I don't need anybody to take care of me. Sure, I miss my dad. I always will. But that doesn't mean..."

"Doesn't mean you want one night of love with a stranger," he said grimly. "Of course not. What would be the point of that?" He knew the answer to that. For him it would be a night to remember. To etch into his subconscious. To keep him going when he was overworked and overtired; for the memories. For her, there was no point. None at all. He should have realized that. She shouldn't have to spell it out for him.

"I'm sorry," he said, seeing the distress on her face. Her fingers continued to work the dough. She gnawed on her lower lip and her eyes were downcast, focused on her work. "You're right, of course. I'm behaving like an adolescent let loose for the first time. You couldn't have made a better diagnosis if you were a psychiatrist."

"Thanks." She looked up and gave him a weak smile.

He grabbed a kitchen chair and straddled it. "Your diagnosis was right on, Doc. I have a case of arrested development complicated by an overactive libido and a vivid imagination. I'm in a place I couldn't have imagined with a woman I never knew existed. And you're right, I don't know the rules here. But you do. What do you recommend? Is there any hope for me? Is there a cure for what ails me?"

Her lips curved. A small dimple flickered at the corner of her mouth. It was a good thing he was sitting down because that smile robbed him of the strength he needed to stand up.

Expertly she stretched the dough into a large rectangle, spread it with butter, raisins and cinnamon and shaped it into individual rolls in a large pan. Then she covered it with a small dish towel. He watched, fascinated. She appeared to have forgotten his question. It was just as well. There was no good answer.

"I've never seen anything like this," he said.

"What, my making rolls? Come on. I guess you never watch the food channel or any cooking shows."

"Hardly. I never watch anything at all. When I get

home from the hospital I fall asleep before I even get to my bedroom. On the couch, in a chair, wherever.''

She leaned back against the counter and met his gaze. ''That kind of life can't be good for you.''

''It won't last forever, although...'' Although his father's life had always been work, work and more work ever since Matt could remember. Not that he didn't enjoy it. He loved it. ''What about that cure?'' he reminded her.

''A cure for an overactive libido?'' she said. ''Sometimes there's nothing you can do but wait for the symptoms to go away.''

''You read that in a book, didn't you?'' he asked. ''Do you really think time will cure what ails me?'' he asked. He hoped it would, but he'd never felt this way before. On the other hand, he didn't want her to think he'd completely lost his head. He had a little pride left. Not much, but a little.

''I don't know. Sometimes there are no cures. There are some things you just have to live with.''

''That's not very hopeful,'' he said.

She sighed. ''I'm sorry,'' she said. ''That's the best I can do. I'm tired and I'm going to bed. Tomorrow may look brighter for everyone, for Donny and the weather and you, too.''

''What about those cinnamon rolls?'' he asked.

''They'll rise overnight, then in the morning I'll put them in the oven and they'll be done in time for breakfast. I'm an early riser. I'll be very quiet so as not to disturb you. Will you be all right on the couch?''

''Of course.''

''I'll get you a blanket and pillow.''

They both knew her father's room was unoccupied, but nobody said anything about his sleeping there. He knew he'd be much better off on the couch, even if his knees were permanently bent and the space was so narrow he might roll off from time to time. Anything was better than sleeping across the hall from her. He didn't want to hear her tossing and turning. He didn't want her to hear him pacing the floor.

He didn't want to run into her in the hall. She'd be wearing a nightgown. But what kind? Something warm and practical, he supposed. Something large and flowing and buttoned up to the neck. Or something soft and clinging. He squeezed his eyes shut to block the mental image. It was no use. No matter how he warned himself not to go there, he couldn't think of anything but her. His hands itched to touch that imaginary nightgown, to peel it off her.

He took a deep breath, vowed to take control of his hyperactive imagination and went back to the living room to put another log on the fire, then stood back to watch the flames. He was sure he wouldn't be able to sleep tonight as long as he was anywhere in this house. How could he when his brain wouldn't quit working overtime and every fiber of his body was alert. Force of habit, he told himself. Years of being on call, getting too little sleep and when he did sleep, it was never very deep.

Carrie came back with sheets, blanket and pillow. She set them carefully on the couch instead of handing them to him. She didn't seem to want to get that close to him. He didn't blame her. She probably didn't trust him. She might think he couldn't control himself. But he could. He'd had years of practice of ignoring his impulses. She started up the stairs, then paused and looked over her shoulder at him.

"Matt? Thanks for coming. I really appreciate it. All that talk about you and me? Let's forget it ever happened, okay?" Her tone was brisk. He had no reason to doubt her sincerity.

He shrugged as if it was no big deal. Forget about it? No problem. If she could forget about it, so could he. Deep down he knew there was no way he'd ever forget anything about her. Even if he left at dawn tomorrow. Even if he married Mira tomorrow. Even if he underwent a course in behavior modification or hypnosis, whatever. As she said, there were some things you just had to live with.

Carrie lay in her bed unable to sleep. She hadn't lied when she said she was tired. Her whole body cried out for sleep, but her brain was racing, replaying every word Matt had said, every gesture he'd made. Her lips stung from his kisses; her skin felt as if it was on fire. She was just as good at diagnosing her own problems as she was Matt's. She knew exactly what was wrong with her, and she had no intention of letting it get the best of her.

She only had to use her willpower and build up her immune system. Today she'd been vulnerable, she'd been weak, she'd allowed herself to give in to her emotions, but only temporarily. Tomorrow she'd be strong. Tomorrow he might be gone. If not, she'd go about her life as if he weren't here. She had the library, she had her friends in the village, she had her boat and her plane and…and…what else? There must be more. She wanted more. She wanted so much more. God help her, she wanted him.

The last time this happened, when she'd fallen for someone almost as unattainable as Matt, she'd fooled herself into thinking it would work out. He would learn to love it in the bush. He'd adapt to her way of life, even though it was completely unreasonable to think so. Hadn't her own mother walked out on her and her father because she couldn't stand the isolation?

This time she was smart enough to know it would never work. She knew this was just a crush on the most attractive man she'd ever met. She knew how to get over it. There was time. There was work. There was...oh, there must be something else.

She heard water running downstairs. She pictured Matt in the kitchen getting a drink. Was he hungry? Did he want some tea, hot chocolate? Was he still wearing her father's clothes or...

She turned over and hit the pillow with her forehead. She strained to hear something from downstairs. There was silence. She could not, should not, must not go down there. His words came back to torture her.

Make love to you on that fur rug in front of the stove...see your skin by firelight, see the flames reflected in your eyes...your hair...

No, she couldn't do this. She had to think of something else. She had to forget what he'd said to her. She had to forget that hungry look in his eyes. The desire that flared and matched hers. The harder she tried to sleep, the more elusive sleep became. She turned over and looked at the clock. Almost midnight. She squeezed her eyes shut. She told herself she had to sleep. The tension of making an effort turned into a headache. She went to the bathroom but couldn't find the aspirin.

She tiptoed down the stairs. If he was asleep, she'd tiptoe right back up. He wasn't asleep. He was sitting on the edge of the couch, leaning forward, his head in his hands. When she realized he was wearing a white T-shirt and boxer shorts, she quickly turned around to go back upstairs. There was just so much she could take.

He looked up when he heard the stairs creak. She paused. His face was half in shadows. She could barely see his eyes, but in the flickering light from the fire she could see something in his gaze that held her there like a prisoner.

"I...I have a little headache," she said. "I came down to get an aspirin."

"Come here," he said. "I have a cure for headaches."

She knew she shouldn't listen. She knew she should just go back upstairs and forget the headache, but there was no way she could ignore him or pretend she hadn't heard. She couldn't imagine his patients ignoring his orders, either. When he said come here in that certain way he had, she had no choice but to obey and come.

He told her to sit on the floor with her back against the couch and rest her head between his knees. She was too tired to protest that she wasn't dressed and thus at risk, and to make matters worse, he was in his underwear. She was too tired to ask what the cure was. If he said he had a cure, he must have one. They were alone, half dressed, miles from anywhere. The air in the room was filled with tension as thick as the fog outside. Whatever happened here would stay in this room. But nothing was going to happen. She'd only known him for a number of hours, but somehow she knew she could trust him implicitly. It was herself she couldn't trust.

He put his hands on the sides of her head and used his strong fingers to massage her temples and knead the back of her neck. She felt the air whoosh out of her lungs and the tension flow out of her head. Her skin tingled. Then he laced his fingers through her hair, sifting the tendrils between his fingers. The fire in the woodstove had burned down to embers. As the stove cooled down, her body felt as if it was on fire. She moaned softly.

"Is that better?" he asked in a deep, slow voice.

"Mmm," she said, her head nestled between his muscular thighs. Her lips were numb. She couldn't form any words. She couldn't even think of any words to express how she felt because she'd never felt this way before. She could stay there forever, as limp as a rag doll with every hormone raging, if it weren't for that warning voice inside her head, the one that asked her if she knew what she was doing.

The answer was no, she didn't. She braced her hands on the floor and tried to get up. She couldn't. He reached down and pulled her up. She didn't dare look at him. Instead she walked to the stairs and without a backward glance she took the stairs one at a time, her legs wobbling, gripping the banister so tightly her knuckles were white.

She tumbled into her bed and fell asleep immediately. The next thing she knew she heard banging in the distance and smelled coffee. She reached for the wind-up clock on her bedside stand and held it in front of her face. Eight-thirty. She never slept past six. She grabbed her long flannel robe and ran down the stairs. Not only did she smell coffee, she smelled cinnamon rolls. How could that be? Where was Matt? Who was at the door?

"Hello, Carrie." Merry Munger stood at the doorway, her short, round body encased in a yellow slicker and knee-high rubber boots on her stubby feet. "Just wanted to see if you were okay," she said peering around the corner into the living room. "Heard you got company."

"That's right," she said, stuffing her arms into the sleeves of her robe. "The doctor who came to see Donny. I couldn't fly him back last night, so he had to stay."

"Mmm-hmm," Merry said. She glanced up at the sky. "Doesn't look like flying weather today, either."

Carrie scanned the gray sky, measuring the low overcast. Her father had taught her so much about the weather up here, she almost didn't need to listen to the forecast. She would have been surprised if it had cleared, since the winds were from the northwest.

"I hear your friend is one young, good-looking fellow," Merry said.

"Really?" Carrie said. Of course word would have gotten out by now. She could just hear the gossips. "You know he's really not my friend. He's a doctor. I never met him before yesterday, and when he leaves, today or tomorrow, I'll never see him again."

"So you say," Merry said. Her wrinkled face broke into a broad smile. "Hello there," she said.

Carrie whirled around. Matt was standing behind her, looming over her shoulder.

"Merry, this is Dr. Baker. Merry runs the country store. Merry, if you'll excuse me, I've got to get dressed. I'm planning to open the library this morning."

"I'll let everyone know," Merry said to Carrie, but her eyes never left Matt's face as she backed down the sidewalk toward her car. What she would let everyone know was that she'd actually seen the young, good-looking doctor and he was every bit as handsome as she'd heard. And that when she'd arrived, Carrie was in her bathrobe and looked as if she'd just gotten up. Not that she would draw any conclusions from that. Oh, no.

Carrie closed the door and leaned back against it. "I can't believe I slept so late," she said, running her hand through her tousled hair. She must look a wreck while Matt looked wide-awake and fresh in a clean pair of khakis and another of her father's shirts. Obviously, he'd been upstairs while she was asleep. He might have taken a shower and found clean clothes and she'd never heard a thing. "I'm usually up at six-thirty. It must have been that headache cure. I was unconscious the minute my head hit the pillow. You ought to bottle it and sell it instead of tranquilizers. I'm going up to get dressed. Did you—" She took a deep breath and told herself to stop rattling on and on. "Do I smell coffee and rolls?" she asked, sniffing the air hungrily.

"You said you were going to put them in the oven, so I did it for you. I hope you don't mind. I have no idea if I did it right or not. I just thought I'd get the jump on you.'' He paused and smiled at her.

Her heart lurched at the way the smile lit his face. Who needed sun shining on southeast Alaska with a man like him around? ''You made the coffee, too,'' she said, returning his smile. Was this what it was like to live with someone who looked like a TV doctor? One who knew how to give massages and start the coffee?

Would you wake up every day feeling like it was the first day of the rest of your life, that life was full of the most amazing possibilities just because he was there smiling at you? She told herself there were no guarantees. Look at her father and mother. They'd been madly in love. They'd probably had days when they felt just like she did right now. And it all turned to dust. ''Are you trying to make me feel inadequate?'' she asked lightly.

''I'm trying to earn my keep. I don't want you to throw me out on the street.''

''No chance,'' she said. ''You treat our patients, make breakfast and give massages like a pro. Where did you learn how to do that?'' She kept her tone casual although she was conscious that her robe was hanging open, exposing her flannel granny gown. Other women her age wore silky gowns with spaghetti straps they ordered from Victoria's Secret. Not her. Maybe if she'd been expecting someone. Maybe if she had someone to wear them for. But she didn't. Matt didn't care what she wore as long as she got him back to his ship and his parents and his girlfriend.

She wasn't usually self-conscious about how she looked. Maybe other women would curl their hair and put on makeup before coming downstairs, but what was the point if no one saw you. When she heard the knocking, she'd rushed to the door. Now it was too late. He'd seen her at her worst, with her hair uncombed and her face unwashed.

He, on the other hand, was wearing a blue chambray work shirt that looked familiar and made him look as if he belonged here. Obviously, he'd been up for a long time. What did he think of her, lazing about in bed that way? She was so embarrassed she ought to run upstairs and get dressed. But she didn't. For some reason her feet wouldn't move.

She stood there gaping at him and let her gaze drift to his mouth. No, she mustn't look at his mouth, mustn't remember how he'd kissed her and how she'd kissed him back. Mustn't wonder how it would feel to kiss him again this morning.

The memories of the night before came wafting through the air like the smell of the hot rolls. Both were impossible to ignore. She dropped her gaze from his face and fiddled with the sash on her robe.

"The massage?" he said. "Believe it or not, I made it up as I went along. That was the first one I've ever given."

"If it was the first, I'm sure it won't be the last. I mean...I didn't mean that I...that you...I just meant you're so good at it you should..."

"I know what you meant," he said, his mouth quirked up at the corners. She was afraid he did know.

"I'll be down in a few minutes," she said as she escaped toward the stairs. "After breakfast I want to head for town and open the library."

"While you're there, I'll go see Donny."

"Matt." She paused and looked out the window at the low overcast. "I'm afraid we won't get out today." She held her breath. Even though she'd tried to prepare him for this eventuality, he might not take it well.

He shrugged. "That's what I figured," he said. "I'll call the ship later and let them know."

Carrie breathed a sigh of relief and went upstairs to get dressed in something more flattering than a billowing nightgown her grandmother might have worn, put on the kind of makeup that didn't look like she was wearing makeup and comb her hair. Not that she hoped Matt would notice. She just felt the need to pull herself together, both internally and externally.

Chapter Four

The library was located in an old house built sometime before statehood in the center of town. The yellow and white Victorian-style building recently repainted by a committee of volunteers also housed the historical museum in one wing and a resale shop in another room. Carrie unlocked the door to the museum, then greeted the man who was working in the shop. He looked up from a pile of old clothes he was sorting.

"Hi, there, Carrie," he said. "Hear you got a doctor for us."

"Just temporarily," she said.

"Oh? I was hoping he was going to stay," he said.

Hoping he was going to stay? Oh, no. Outsiders don't stay. Don't even think about it. "No, Mac, he's only here for a day or two, to do what he can for Donny. He's a city doctor, a plastic surgeon who's on vacation. He was good enough to come here without notice when I told him about the emergency."

"What's he say about the boy?" Mac asked, peering at her through his bifocals.

"He thinks he's stabilized. I'm hopeful I got him

here in time to stop the swelling and hopefully limit the amount of injury. But it's impossible to tell without an X ray and a scan or an MRI, and they are only available at a hospital somewhere.''

''So why don't you fly Donny out to a hospital, Fairbanks or somewhere?''

''Yes, I will, or someone will. But he shouldn't be moved until he's better. And another thing, I can't fly anywhere in this weather. Which is why the doctor is still around.''

''Hear he's staying with you,'' he said. Carrie wasn't sure, but she thought there was a hint of speculation in the old man's eyes.

''Well, yes,'' she said. ''I've got room and he doesn't know anyone else in town.''

''What do you think of him?'' Mac asked.

''What do I think? I think he's incredibly generous to interrupt his vacation to come here and take a look at Donny. From what I can tell, he seems to be a very good doctor. I think we're very lucky to have him.''

''Big-city doc, you say?'' he said.

''Yes.'' She had the feeling this conversation could go on all day if she let it. So she excused herself and went to open the library door. The minute she did, the phone rang. It had nothing to do with books, it was someone asking about the doctor. She told the caller, a fisherman known as Smoky Joe, just what she'd told Mac, only a more abbreviated form. Then the customers came. At first she thought it was the weather that caused everyone to turn to books for entertainment, but after the first few patrons had come in, she realized it was curiosity that brought them.

She was irritated at first, but realized she couldn't

blame them. Life in their little town could get dull, especially under leaden skies, with no mail delivery to look forward to. She'd brought in some excitement in the form of a doctor, and he was fair game as an object of curiosity. And of course everyone was worried about Donny. Though it seemed that everyone had already called over to his house to get the latest update on his condition.

"I hear they're playing chess," Allison Rathman told Carrie, leaning against a bookcase. Allison was a high school girl, the star of the girls' basketball team.

"Who's playing chess?" Carrie asked, as she stamped the return date on a book about raising parakeets for Marge Seton.

"Donny and the doctor," Allison said. "You know how Donny was always wanting somebody to play with him? Well, looks like he found somebody."

"I can't believe Donny's feeling well enough to play chess," Carrie murmured. The boy had learned on his own, from books Carrie had ordered for him from the state library service. Occasionally somebody would drift through town and play with him and give him a few pointers. But yesterday he'd been flat on his back. How could he be well enough to move the pieces around? Was this just another rumor or was Dr. Matt really able to perform miracles? He'd certainly done a job on her aching head last night. She felt a tiny shiver go up her spine, thinking of the way his hands felt releasing tension from muscles and causing her to feel as if every bone in her body had turned to jelly.

"…another mystery by that writer, you know who I mean?"

Carrie looked up, aware that she'd been daydreaming, and met the inquiring gaze of Maggie Cummings. She got up from behind her desk and went back to the small mystery section with Maggie. It was a relief to discuss books for a change. She was able to steer Maggie to a couple of writers she thought she'd like. But there was no escaping her questions about the new man in town. After she'd filled her arms with a selection of books, Maggie leaned forward and asked the questions that were on everyone's mind today.

"Where on earth did you find that man?" she asked breathlessly. "He's gorgeous."

"How did you…I mean how do you know?" Carrie asked.

"Peeked in the window over at the house," she confessed, her high cheekbones expertly tinged with pink. Even when she was just taking a walk to the mailbox, Maggie was perfectly made-up, which made her stand out from 99 percent of the local population. "I guess I shouldn't have, but I couldn't resist. How many times does a new man come to town? I didn't want to bother anyone by knocking on the front door. There he was, sitting by Donny's bed, the chess board between them. I couldn't believe it."

"So it's true," Carrie said.

"Oh, yes, it's true. He's the best-looking man to hit this town in ten years. No, make that this whole territory. I ought to know. But, tell me, is he married?"

Carrie shook her head. She could have told Maggie

about his girlfriend, but that wouldn't have slowed Maggie down one bit.

Maggie breathed an exaggerated sigh of relief. "But you've got first dibs on him, Carrie. You saw him first," she said.

"What?" Carrie backed into a bookshelf. "Wait a minute. Sure, I saw him first, but I'm only interested in him as a doctor, nothing else," she said, hoping Maggie couldn't see her blush.

"Well, if you're sure. But really, Carrie, you're passing up a good bet. It's about time you woke up and smelled the roses, if you get what I mean. If I'd let one rotten man spoil my view of the whole species, where would I be now?"

Carrie shook her head as if she didn't know the answer. But she did. It was obvious that Maggie would be where Carrie was, alone and destined to stay alone, fulfilling her father's hopes and dreams, while Maggie was out flirting with every man who came within her territory, by boat or plane. She had no hang-ups about loving and leaving any man who crossed her path. Carrie guessed that was one way of getting through the long, cold winters. It just wasn't her way.

Even though she wouldn't say it, Carrie had to agree that not only was Matt the best-looking man to hit the town in ten years, but also that Maggie ought to know. She'd been looking for a man ever since her husband walked out and went back to the lower forty-eight, something fairly rare. Usually it was the woman who couldn't take the isolation, the lack of amenities and the cool, rainy weather. It wasn't only Carrie's mother who'd gone home after a few years in the bush. She was just one of many.

But Maggie loved living in the bush. She knew how to use a chain saw and a fishing rod, all without smudging her mascara. She, too, had her own boat and made the rounds of the other villages along the waterfront, visiting friends and buying native crafts. She had her own Internet business selling moccasins and beaded necklaces and carvings from her Web site. Her whole house was full to the brim with artifacts. At the moment she was wearing a carved soapstone pendant and a shell bracelet, all part of her collection.

Though she'd reputedly had many romances with various men over the years, from one-night stands to several-month stands, it seemed Maggie hadn't yet found anybody to take Bud's place. She was convinced it was just a matter of time. After all, the ratio of men to women in the state was twenty-five to one. Of course, the saying up there was that though the odds were good, the goods were odd. Maybe Maggie didn't want anyone around permanently. Maybe she liked the variety of a new man every few months or whenever they happened along. Carrie had never talked to her about such things.

No wonder Maggie had her eye on Dr. Matt. He was single. He was a professional. He was far from odd. Surely Carrie didn't have to warn Maggie that Matt was not going to be around for more than a day or two. Maybe that's all she wanted. Maybe she didn't care that this was somebody with whom she could have no future.

In Carrie's view, nobody in their right mind would fall for a doctor who didn't belong up here. Having a short-term affair with someone you'd never see again would be the height of folly as far as she was concerned. These were thoughts Carrie kept to herself. She was hardly one to give advice. She'd fallen for someone who didn't belong up there and tried to convince herself he did. Maggie knew that. The whole town knew it. It was hard to keep a secret in Mystic, population 325.

After she found a book for Maggie, and Maggie sat down in the large, comfortable, overstuffed chair that Carrie had donated to the library, Carrie helped some students do research for a paper they were writing for school. When Matt walked in an hour later, a hush fell over the library. Everyone looked up from the book or magazine or newspaper or encyclopedia they were reading. He stood in the doorway for a moment, and she was struck again by how he'd taken on the look of a true Alaskan in less than twenty-four hours. Not that he'd grown a beard or carried a pickax; it was more subtle than that. It was something about the expression on his face. Yesterday he'd been a tourist, today he looked as though he fitted in. Not that he really did. She cautioned herself against even thinking such a thing.

Maybe it was the fact that instead of his Yuppie brand-name clothes, he was wearing her father's well-washed chambray shirt and khakis. He stood in the doorway, momentarily surprised at the reception he'd received. He shouldn't be surprised, Carrie thought. By now he should know he had reached near celebrity status in town.

"Come in," she said, getting up from her desk. "Come and meet the library patrons."

She introduced him to the dozen or so citizens who shook his hand and thanked him for coming and then let him answer the question that was on everyone's mind. How's Donny?

He sat on the edge of Carrie's desk and explained what spinal-cord trauma was, the causes and the effect and the possible outcome of such injury. He also talked about how to prevent such accidents as Donny had had.

"Football and sledding injuries sometimes involve abnormal twisting and bending of the back or neck, like this." He twisted his body to simulate a sports injury which was more effective than a picture. There was a chorus of oohs and aahs in the room. "When you do go sledding," he added, "inspect the area for obstacles. Any bumps or holes can cause you to fly off your sled and hit your head or your spine. Always wear a helmet and other protective gear when you're playing football or even sledding. ATVs are especially dangerous. They don't have the stability of a four-wheel vehicle. If you must drive one, then, again, wear a helmet.

"Most spinal-cord injuries like Donny's happen to young males between the ages of fifteen and thirty-five. But they can be prevented if you use the proper equipment and follow safety rules."

The boys in the group nodded soberly. Some were Donny's good friends. Carrie hoped they'd follow this good advice. It was painful to think that his accident could have been prevented. But all this was general information, and the crowd wanted specifics. Was their friend going to get well?

Matt explained that he'd done what he could by

giving Donny medicines to reduce the swelling on his spinal cord. Prompt treatment was essential and if it hadn't been for Carrie, there was no telling what the outcome would be. As it was, he couldn't tell for sure, not until Donny had an X ray to see what the damage was. Eventually he'd have to be airlifted out to be treated at a hospital where he might have to have surgery. Matt said it was quite possible the boy would recover completely. In the meantime they could visit him, as long as they didn't get him too tired.

Carrie admired his patience as Matt sat there until every question had been answered. Not only would he make a good doctor, she had the feeling he'd be good at teaching medicine if that was what he wanted to do. Finally Donny's friends drifted out and the library atmosphere returned to somewhat normal. Carrie answered the phone while Matt walked between the stacks and examined the books. It must look terribly inadequate and meager to him. He couldn't know how she'd begged, borrowed and bought books with her own money to fill the shelves. She was proud of it. It was not only a place to find information or entertainment between the pages of a book, it was also a place for townspeople to gather to exchange news and information, especially at a time like this where one of their own was in danger.

Out of the corner of her eye she saw Maggie, who'd been silent during Matt's talk, get up from her chair, tuck her book under her arm and very casually sidle up to him and strike up a conversation. She couldn't hear what they were talking about but she could imagine. Maggie was giving him a dose of Alaska lore. She could understand why Matt might be interested in her. While in her late thirties, she could easily pass for twenty-five with her smooth skin and bright-blue eyes. Carrie could understand why any man would find her attractive. She knew a lot and she'd seen a lot. She liked men and men liked her. Matt was a change from the rugged lumberjacks and fishermen she usually hung out with. She would have noticed by now that he wasn't wearing a wedding ring.

Carrie felt a stab of jealousy watching them talking together. Why should she? He didn't belong to her. If he belonged to anyone, it was to his girlfriend back on the ship. She wondered if he'd called the ship yet and left word he wouldn't be back today. How many more days would he be trapped here?

She hung up without knowing what book she'd promised to look for, and typed out labels on her old manual typewriter for some new books that had arrived. All the while Matt and Maggie were back in the stacks talking in low voices. Finally Maggie walked to the desk to check out her book. Before she left, she paused at the door and turned to wave to Matt.

"See you later," she said. "Let me know if you want to take me up on my offer."

He nodded.

Carrie forced herself to stay calm. Whatever offer she'd made was between them. Carrie should be focusing on the books she was cataloging instead of looking out the window at Maggie, who was walking across the road, her blond hair blowing in the wind. Matt didn't belong to her just because she was the one who'd found him and brought him here. There was no such thing as first dibs as far as she was concerned. Not with people. Especially not with men.

He could see whoever he wanted. No one said he had to spend every minute he wasn't taking care of Donny with her. It was good that he got to meet the locals. Hadn't she wanted to show him it was the friendliest town in the state? Didn't she want him to experience it for himself as a kind of justification for her staying up there? The answers were yes and yes. Of course she did. Then why did she feel so edgy, as if she was sitting on a fence and the slightest breeze would push her over? If she were that fragile, she shouldn't be living in the last frontier. She shouldn't be flying around the state by herself. She should hibernate with the bears for the winter.

It was no use pretending Matt wasn't in the library. Everyone else had left, knowing that she closed at noon. It didn't do any good to imagine this was an ordinary day in the life of a part-time librarian. Even as she typed a label she knew exactly where he was in the stacks. When he came out he was carrying a book about the Russian occupation of Alaska.

"Your friend Maggie was telling me about an island near here where the Russians built a small church. She says you can visit the remains and get a feeling for another era of Alaska history. I had no idea they actually had a colony up here. I thought they'd come and hunted seal and left."

"No, they had many settlements. Not only hunting and fishing, but trading as well. Did she offer to take you to the island in her boat?" Carrie asked. It was hard, but she kept her tone neutral as if it was only of small interest whether she had or not. And even less interest whether he'd accepted her offer. Nevertheless, Matt shot her a surprised glance.

"How did you know?" he asked.

"I told you this was a friendly town. Did you say yes?" she asked.

"I told her I'd let her know. I hate to be a burden on you, and I know you have things to do, but I was hoping I could convince you to take me there."

"Oh." Relief made her light-headed and almost giddy. "Of course I can." She looked up at the gray sky. "I don't think it will rain, at least for a while, so we ought to take advantage of the weather, or lack of weather. What's really happening with Donny?" she asked. "I was surprised to hear he was well enough to play chess."

"So was I. And glad he could sit up today. Chess gave him an incentive to move his upper body a little so we had a few games. He's really very good. He says you got him some books on chess and encouraged him to learn the game."

"Yes, but it's hard to learn from books. I've always wished he had someone to play with. He must be better."

"Somewhat. The medicines I gave him have reduced the pain and the swelling, so at least he feels better. What's really going on is something we won't know until we get him out of here and get some pictures of what's going on inside. But I wouldn't want to chance that for a few weeks." He glanced up at the sky. "Maybe I'll still be here by then."

The thought of Matt staying there for weeks instead of days made her feel panicky. She didn't know how much longer she could be in such close contact with him and not show her feelings. Impulsively she grabbed him by the arm. "Oh, no," she said. "This kind of weather doesn't ever last that long. Aren't you due in San Francisco soon?"

"Next week," he said. "But if I can't get out, I can't get out."

He sounded so philosophical about it she was shocked.

"But they're expecting you. This is a big opportunity for you. Your father told me how competitive these residencies are. You've been chosen. You can't be late."

"It sounds as if you're anxious to get rid of me," he said, helping her on with her jacket. His hands brushed her shoulders, and it seemed they lingered longer than necessary.

"No, of course not. It's just..."

"It's just that I'm cramping your style, aren't I? Don't feel you have to show me around."

She turned to face him. "I want to," she said.

"I want you to," he said.

Her heart skipped a beat. She was glad he wasn't monitoring her pulse at that moment. He was so close she could smell the soap on his hands and the coffee on his breath. She could feel the heat from his body. He was close, but not close enough. She wanted to throw her arms around him, to press her breasts against the muscles in his chest, to feel his heartbeat right through his shirt, to see if it matched her own. She wanted to know if he felt the same as she did.

They stood there in the silence of the library, with the familiar musty smell of old books mingled with the smell of paste and glue, locked in a contest to see who would look away first. It wouldn't be her. She was lost in the depths of his eyes that seemed as dark as the deepest sea.

She didn't know how long they might have stood there while the tension built. They might have been there for hours if it hadn't been for Merry knocking on the door. Carrie started guiltily and stepped backward. The spell was broken. The tension was gone.

"Hello," Merry called gaily. "Are you still there, Carrie? I came to invite you and the doctor to lunch."

Carrie opened the door. Merry stepped in, and her keen, inquisitive gaze shifted from Carrie to Matt and back again. She smiled brightly and repeated her invitation.

Lunch was in Merry's house behind the store. The wall was decorated with antlers from a moose her husband had shot. The heat from her woodstove was welcome after the chill outside. Merry was not only a good cook, but she had access to the best ingredients before her customers did. She also subscribed to a number of cooking magazines. Her dishes were always the first to disappear at any potluck dinner. Today she made puffy crab soufflés and beamed at the compliments she got from her two guests.

"It's not often we have a stranger in town," Merry said, pouring hot coffee into their cups. "I hope you get a chance to see something of this region before you go."

"Carrie has offered to take me out in her boat this afternoon," Matt said.

Merry nodded approvingly. "She knows the area like no one else."

Except for Maggie, Carrie thought. But she didn't say it.

On their way out they ran into Jack, Merry's husband, just back from a fishing trip.

"This is the doctor who's taking care of Donny," Merry explained.

"You missed a great lunch," Carrie told him.

Jack shook Matt's hand and told him how glad they were he'd come to Mystic to see their boy. Then he opened his cooler and showed them his catch—cod, snapper and salmon. He asked if Carrie wanted any, but she said her freezer was full and thanked him anyway.

"You're right," Matt said as they rode to her house, "this must be the friendliest town in Alaska, if not the whole country. I can't believe how you all look after each other. That is a rare thing. No wonder you stay here. I'm not used to being treated like a celebrity. I haven't performed any miracles. You're the one who should be getting all the attention. You're the one who went after help. You talked me into coming and then you flew me here."

She shook her head. "It didn't take much talking before you volunteered. How many doctors would have interrupted their vacation to fly off into the bush? You didn't know me. You had no idea if I was on the level or not. To say nothing of my flying ability. You took a chance coming out here," she said. Her eyes glowed with honest admiration, which he didn't feel he really deserved.

Matt felt embarrassed to be the recipient of all this attention. Of course he was glad to do what he could for Donny and anyone else he could help. He was especially glad to have a chance to try to prevent further spinal-cord injuries. But to be treated like a celebrity made him uncomfortable.

On the other hand he didn't object to being the object of Carrie's admiration whether he deserved it or not. He basked in her approval. It made him feel like the superhero he was not. It made him feel as if he could do anything. Anything except make love to her. That would be wrong. It wasn't what she wanted.

It was what he wanted. He'd wanted it ever since he'd first seen her on the dock, was it only yesterday? It seemed like a lifetime away. Since then he'd been drawn into her life. He'd slept under her roof, he'd worn her father's clothes and he'd eaten her food. And he'd kissed her. He wanted to kiss her now. He wanted to pull off the road so he could put his arms around her, drag her across the seat and devour her.

He slanted his gaze in her direction, studying her profile, the tendrils of red-gold hair that brushed her cheek and the curve of her chin. His fingers itched to cup her face between his hands and kiss her eyelids, her temples, the tender places behind her ears. He wanted to hear her moan, to murmur his name. He wanted…

"What?" she said, turning to meet his gaze. He wondered if he'd spoken aloud or had she just intercepted his thoughts. He wouldn't be surprised. He half wanted her to know how he felt.

But he wasn't ready to say anything now. He shook his head. He knew he hadn't said anything. He looked at her again. Had she read his thoughts? Was he that transparent? Did she really know how he felt? Had she felt the heat of his pent-up passion? Had she felt the vibrations in the air? She may have, because she blushed slightly and turned her attention to the road ahead of her.

"We'll stop by the house and pick up some gear, then drive to the dock and get the boat," Carrie said. "If you're still interested in seeing the islands."

He was. He was interested in seeing every part of her world and meeting everyone in her world. "I'm going to get my camera," he said.

Her boat was docked at the pier in town. It was a small wooden launch with room for four or maybe six passengers in the cabin. He pushed off and jumped in after she'd started the engine. They passed fishing boats coming in with their catches. Everyone yelled back and forth, exchanging news and greetings.

"You know everyone," he said, joining her in the cabin.

"Of course," she said. "So will you in a few days."

"A few days?" he asked. "How much longer do you really think I'll be here?" He had mixed feelings about staying there. On one hand, he knew his parents were missing him. They'd planned this cruise so they could all be together before he started his arduous internship. On the other hand, being here was the experience of a lifetime. Then there was Carrie....

"I don't know." She looked out the Plexiglas window, studying the sky. "There's at least a hundred-foot ceiling of cloud cover hanging over us. I could be wrong, but this kind of cloud bank usually stays around awhile. Oh, not forever. But it looks pretty dense. I'm really sorry, Matt," she said, putting her hand lightly on his arm. "I know what you're giving up. I feel terrible about keeping you from your vacation.''

''My vacation? This is the best vacation I could imagine. Everyone on that ship would give anything for an opportunity like this. Seeing the inside passage of Alaska with an insider. I've never had such a good time.''

She smiled. ''Really?''

''Really.'' Impulsively he leaned toward her and kissed her on the mouth. He tasted coffee and something so sweet he didn't know what to call it. It was the essence of Carrie. He was sorely tempted to coax a kiss out of her, only, he knew once he started, he wouldn't want to stop. Want to? Hell, he wouldn't be able to. He didn't know what had happened to him. He used to be the most self-controlled person in the world. He'd given up every distraction for as long as he could remember to focus on medicine. Suddenly he was giving in to impulses and desires he thought he'd buried long ago. It was intoxicating. It made him feel as if a fifty-pound load had been removed from his shoulders.

But now was not the time to give in to any further impulses. He was going sight-seeing. He called on some of that almost-forgotten discipline. With every bit of strength he could muster he broke away, before he got carried away and did what he wanted to do. He broke away just in time to hear her sigh softly. A sigh of regret? A sigh of longing? Good Lord, what would happen if he was here for many more days? How strong was he? How much temptation could he stand before he caved in? What did she think would happen? What did she want to happen?

To have something else to do, he took out his camera and started taking pictures. Anything to keep his mind off his conflict. He took pictures of the gray-green water of the sound and the spruce trees growing on the banks right down to the water's edge. He took pictures of every bird he could see, whether they were falcons or hawks or maybe even eagles. It didn't matter as long as he captured them on film. He took pictures to keep his hands from reaching for her. But he couldn't stop looking at her.

"What are you doing?" she asked as he turned the camera on her.

"Taking pictures of you."

She ran her hand through her hair. "You should have told me. I look a wreck."

"You look beautiful," he said. He meant it.

She grinned. She didn't believe him, but she accepted the compliment anyway. "Want to steer?" she asked.

"Sure." He traded places with her.

"Just stay within the markers," she said. "We're heading east around the next bend." She picked up his camera and focused it on him. "How do you like being the subject?" she asked.

"Fine with me," he said. "I know what you want. A picture of me to remember me by. Don't worry, I'll send you copies."

"You think I'll need a picture to remember you?"

He turned to face her, his hands on the steering wheel. He didn't want her to forget him. He didn't want her to need a picture. He wanted her to think about him as often as he was sure he was going to think about her. He didn't want to be the only one to look back on this big adventure in his life and re-member what it was like to feel this heightened awareness of everything and everybody. This feeling that every minute was precious. The air was charged with so much electricity he expected a spontaneous explosion to occur any minute.

He'd never felt so close to another person. So close he felt as if he'd known her all his life. And yet he didn't know her at all. Not yet.

"I don't know," he said soberly. "I know I'll never forget you. Never forget this time we've spent together. For me, every minute is precious. Every bird, every tree is different from anything I've seen before. Those mountains in the distance, the water, the town—" he took a deep breath and went on even though he might be sorry later "—and you, you're not like anyone I've ever met before."

She didn't answer. She bit her lip and turned to look out the window. He didn't know if he'd offended her or not. Maybe he should have kept his mouth shut.

"I haven't met many future plastic surgeons, ei-ther," she said. "So we're even."

"That's not exactly what I meant," he said. "And I think you know it."

"All right, plastic surgeon or tree surgeon, you're different from anyone I've ever met," she admitted. "And I won't forget you, either."

Chapter Five

Matt was touched by Carrie's words. More than touched, he was warmed. Clear down to the toes in his boots. He didn't say anything. He just let the words hang in the air—*I won't forget you, either*—until he handed over the controls to Carrie in midstream before they got to the island. He stood outside on the deck and watched admiringly as she expertly edged the launch up to the side of an old wooden dock. Then he jumped out and wrapped the rope around a post. He held out his hand to grab her as she jumped down to the rickety dock. There were boards missing so he opened his arms to catch her just in case. It wasn't a rational decision to put his arms around her and hug her tightly, it just happened. They both let go at the same time, as if they'd shared the same thought, the same warning. Be careful. Not just of rotten boards, but of passion out of control. Keep your distance. This was happening too fast. Much too fast.

"This is it," she said, with a wide gesture as they stepped off the dock onto the muddy ground. "St. Elias Island, or as the natives called it, Yukatak Island. There's not much left except the church. But that's worth the trip all by itself. At least I think so.''

Carrie led the way down a narrow winding path overgrown with brambles that tore at their clothes as they walked single file toward the church. The crows overhead screamed at them as if to warn the forest creatures of their arrival. Once she reached back with her hand and he took it. He loved the way she walked, with a confident spring in her step. He loved the way her hair brushed her shoulders, a bright flame of color in the gray misty air. He loved the way her hips swayed in her brown corduroy slacks. Was there anything about her he didn't love?

They walked that way, single file, but hand in hand until they reached the clearing where the remains of the church stood. He stopped dead in his tracks and stared at the four standing walls made of logs. The roof had fallen in, but the rotten roof beams were still there, resting against the walls as if a giant had been playing with his toy house and had suddenly abandoned it for something more interesting.

''This is amazing,'' he said.

She nodded, smiling, pleased at his approval. ''Wait till you see the inside.''

Though the roof was gone and whitewashed walls were cracked and gray, he still knew he was in a church. A hush had fallen over the forest. Even the birds were quiet. There were pictures painted on the walls, faded, but still beautiful, one of a Madonna, others of various saints whose names he didn't know.

Carrie didn't say anything. She hoped he'd appreciate it as much as she did, but that was asking a lot. This had always been her special spot. Not just hers, of course. Others came here. Maggie came here. But as president of the historical society of Mystic, it held a special spot in her heart.

She'd never brought anyone here before, not even her fiancé. She stood back and let Matt discover the church by himself. He walked around and exclaimed at the candle stubs in metal holders and at the altar made of old fir. She wondered if he could picture an old Russian priest standing there, ringing the bell, giving communion from a brass cup to a ragtag collection of Russian fur traders and Native Americans.

"Is it ever used anymore?" he asked.

She shook her head. "I don't think so. But at one time both native people and Russians worshipped here together."

Matt examined an intricately carved wooden cabinet inlaid with mother-of-pearl that stood in the corner. He tried the door, but it was locked.

"Too bad it won't open," she said. "I've always wanted to know what's inside."

"Shall I try?" he asked.

She nodded.

He took his Swiss Army knife from his pocket and after gently working at the lock for a few minutes, it sprung open. She drew a quick breath of surprise. Then she reached in and brought out an old Russian Bible written in Cyrillic. They both stood staring at the gold writing on the black leather cover, then very carefully Carrie set it on the altar. Her hands shook with excitement. It was very old, almost two hundred years old, she thought. She turned a few pages, each the thickness of tissue.

A thin piece of paper fluttered out.

"It looks like a marriage certificate," she said, running her finger over two very official-looking stamps on it. Two names were inscribed both in Russian script and in English. "These must be the bride and groom. I can't believe this," Carrie said, her voice tinged with awe. "Though I shouldn't be surprised. Marriages between local people and the Russians were not uncommon. In fact, there are some in our village who claim to be part Russian."

"So the Russians integrated themselves into local society."

"Or vice versa," she said. "The local people integrated themselves into Russian society."

"What must the Indians have thought of them with their strange customs and weird clothes?"

"Imagine what the Russians thought of our Indians who knew how to catch fish with their hands and cook it over hot coals the way we still do today. They knew where the best bushberries were and the wild onions and how to make spears from stone."

"They must have learned a lot from each other."

"When they weren't fighting," she said dryly. "In any case, I would love to have seen this wedding. Imagine her in her soft leather dress made of the finest skins decorated with beads made of stone or shells. Imagine him in his beard and uniform. From his title here I gather he must have been a naval officer."

"It looks like no one uses the church anymore," he said.

"No, especially not for weddings," she said. "But from here you can see…" She looked off into the distance. "On a clear day you could see the water and the mountains. Maybe it was clear the day they were married. Maybe the guests threw rice at them, if that was their custom, maybe they drank homemade wine made of fermented berries, or vodka imported from the old country.''

"Maybe you'd like to be married here someday," he suggested.

"Me?" The suggestion broke into her reverie and forced her back to the present. "Oh, no. I don't plan on getting married. Or getting rained on while I get married," she said lightly. She glanced up at the open roof above them. She avoided his gaze by studying the Bible. She didn't want him to know about her broken engagement. That she'd once planned a wedding that never happened. It was too humiliating. Not that she'd been dumped, but that she'd been so wrong to think anybody would want to give up life on the outside for a life with her in the bush.

"Why not get married? There must be plenty of men up here who are after you."

"There have been a few," she admitted, taking the Bible and putting it back into the cupboard. "But no one I wanted to spend the rest of my life with. Some people think I'm being too choosy, but really I'm happy with my life as it is. In a way, I'm married to my job. That's what my dad used to say. You may not believe this, seeing me take time off this way, but I'm usually busy, flying around the state."

"What, no time for sight-seeing?" he asked.

"Sight-seeing is more fun when you have someone to show the sights to," she said.

"I appreciate your taking time off to show me around. The eagles' nests and this and your town. I feel...lucky."

"Lucky? Lucky that I interrupted your vacation? Lucky that you're stuck here in the bush with nothing to do?"

He tilted her chin with his thumb and forced her to look in his eyes. Dark eyes so deep she was afraid to get lost in their depths. She licked her lips nervously, hoping he couldn't read her thoughts. Hoping he couldn't know that she could never marry anyone who didn't make her feel the way he did. That he was going to spoil her for anyone else who might come along. That if she was choosy before she met him, she would be more so after he left.

"Lucky that I met you," he said. He smiled and her heart caught in her throat. She knew what had to come next. If he didn't kiss her, she would kiss him. It didn't matter, she just had to feel his mouth on hers. She wanted his arms around her, pulling her close. She wanted to stop talking about the past or the future. She wanted to live in the present for only a few hours or a few days. She would deal with the future later.

She knew this wasn't going to last. She knew he was going to leave. It didn't take a rocket scientist to know it would never work. This time when she looked in his eyes she saw a flash of white-hot desire that matched her own. He angled his face and kissed her just as it started to rain.

She felt his lips curve against hers as the rain came down through the open roof and soaked them in earnest. She tasted the fresh rainwater on his lips, then she ran her hands through his wet hair, loving the feel of the thick wet strands on her fingers. Her wet shirt was plastered against his. She could feel the muscles of his chest pressed against her breasts, almost as if there was no barrier between them. His lips found the indentation in her throat and she couldn't control herself. She moaned, she sighed, she gasped. She wanted him. She wanted him so badly. But not here, not in the church. Not in the rain.

"Let's get out of here," she said, pulling away.

They ran back down the path, hand in hand, muddy banks on either side, their shoes sinking into the dense carpet of fallen needles at least a foot thick. Their feet made soft crunching sounds as they ran. She got into the boat first, a custom that was becoming a habit, and he pushed off as he'd been doing. He shook the water off his clothes and his hair before he got into the cabin with her.

She looked at him and burst into laughter. "You look like a wet dog," she said.

He sat next to her and ran his fingers through her hair, sending a spray of water onto her shoulders. "What kind?" he asked.

"A husky, of course."

"And you, you look like a golden Lab." The look he gave her was amused but so tender it made it hard to catch her breath.

A laugh caught in her throat. She shivered, both from the cold and from his touch.

"Where are those hot springs you told me about?" he asked. "I could use a hot bath right now."

She started the engine. "Not too far." She hesitated only a moment. Only long enough to think about taking off her clothes and soaking with him. This was no time to get modest. No time to call a halt to what was inevitable. She was falling in love with another unavailable, unattainable man. She was falling in love with Matt. She wanted to make love to him. She must not make love to him. If she did, she'd be sorry for the rest of her life. Trying to balance the conflict in her mind made her head hurt. She told herself to give up trying. This was not the time to be reasonable. This was a once-in-a-lifetime situation with a once-in-a-lifetime man.

She sent the launch hurtling through the water at full speed before she could change her mind. At that rate, they reached the hot springs island twenty minutes later. Instead of a dock, there was a sandy spit to pull the boat up onto. Leaving the boat behind them on the spit, they started up a steep winding path.

''I've got some dry clothes in the hatch for later. Seemed crazy to change now, but later after we get out…'' She didn't say where or how they'd change. She didn't say how they'd get into the pool of hot water without taking their clothes off and going in naked. The rain came down harder, her hair stuck to the back of her neck, her shirt stuck to her skin. Water ran down her legs into her shoes. She walked faster, becoming totally soaked, but she didn't care. She had a feeling Matt didn't, either.

Matt's heart was pounding in his chest. Not from the steep walk along the creek, but from the possibility of what was to come. The scenarios played out in front of his mind like a movie. Carrie floating in the hot water, steam billowing, partly obscuring her body. He'd come up behind her, cup her breasts with his hands… Was that what she wanted, too? Was that why she'd brought him there? If it wasn't, he was in for a major disappointment. All he could do was to wait and see.

The vapor was rising from the stream as they neared the pools. The gray-green water was getting warmer and warmer as they climbed. The rain slowed to a drizzle.

She paused by the edge of the pond and gazed into the clear waters of the pool. "Is this crazy or what?" she asked him. "We're already soaked."

"We're soaked, but we're not hot," he said, trying to sound reasonable when he felt anything but. He was afraid if either one thought about it, hesitated only a moment, the moment would be lost. They'd lose their nerve, turn around and go back and never have this chance again. He peeled his wet shirt off and tossed it on the ground.

"Last one in is a monkey's uncle," he said. That's right, make light of it, he told himself. Pretend your heart isn't in your throat. Pretend this is all light-hearted fun. That it doesn't matter.

She turned her back on him and disappeared behind a tree. He piled his clothes in a heap on a rock and slid into the water. He gasped. It was hot. It was waist deep.

"Close your eyes," she said from behind the tree. "I'm coming in."

Reluctantly he closed his eyes and turned around so he wouldn't see her. The next thing he heard was a splash. Then a gasp.

"I forgot how hot it was."

"That's the idea, isn't it?" he asked. How long could he keep his back turned. How long would he have to imagine how she looked. How long before he could actually see her? Never?

"Okay," she said, as if she'd heard his questions. "You can turn around now."

All he could see was her head, her hair dark and wet, her eyes huge in her face. She'd sunk down so the rest of her body was covered with water and obscured by the steam. But if he looked carefully… No, he would not look carefully. He looked away. Following her example, he sank into the water, so that he too was covered except for his head.

"Is this where you saw the bear?" he asked, turning his head toward the rocky shore.

She raised her hand and pointed to a stand of fir trees. "He came from over there."

"What happened?"

"I scared him away."

"You scared a bear? How did you do that?" he asked.

"Well, I stood up and waved my arms and yelled and started wading toward the shore."

He took a deep breath. "I wish I'd been there," he muttered. He would have chanced being eaten by a bear for a glimpse of her body rising out of the steam. "So if it happens again, can I count on you to save us?" he asked.

"Oh, sure, no problem. But you'll have to promise to close your eyes."

"Carrie, I'm a doctor. I've seen naked bodies before." *But I've never seen yours before, and I want to. I want to more than you know. I want to so badly it hurts.* He stood, waist deep in the water, and walked toward her slowly. Giving her time to back up, to move away, to show by the look in her eyes that she wanted to keep her distance.

His body felt heavy and clumsy in the hot water. She watched him without moving, without blinking. Her eyes were glazed with what he hoped was desire. When he got close he held out his arms, and she stood and walked into them as if she was going home. Without a moment's hesitation. Her body was slick and hot and he was afraid he was going to pass out from the sheer ecstasy of holding her in his arms.

He caught only a glimpse of her full, rose-tipped breasts before he pressed them against his chest. He ran one hand through her dark, tangled hair and brought her face to his so he could kiss her again and again.

They sank down together into the water, their knees on the sandy bottom of the pool, her breasts floating near the surface. He tried to steady his breathing, but couldn't. He leaned forward, cupped her breasts in his hands and took one nipple at a time into his mouth. She let her head fall backward as she murmured something he couldn't understand. It could have been his name, it could have been a protest or it could have been a primal sound of surrender. Her breasts swelled in his hands, filling them. He didn't plan to make love to her here, but he didn't know how much longer he could wait.

Her arms slid around his waist. Her eyes were closed. Her lips parted. The rain had stopped. When it had happened he had no idea. Every one of his senses was filled with her. The smell of her hair, the taste of her skin, the sound of her heart beating. The water that surrounded them and made them one. That was what he wanted. To be one with her. To give her everything he had. His heart, his soul, his body and to take everything in return. Her heart, her soul and her body.

He knew it wasn't the time or place for that. Even though his brain had turned to mush in the hot steam, he was alert enough to know that much. He could almost count the reasons why it wasn't.

"Carrie," he blurted. "I want to make love to you." As if she hadn't noticed. It was obvious. Still, he had to say it. He had to give her a chance to tell him why not. They'd be the same as his reasons. Wrong time, wrong place, wrong person, and finally—no future.

She nodded. "I know." Her voice was breathless. He wanted her to say yes or no. He wanted her to make the decision. "Not now," she said at last in a throaty whisper. "Later."

Later. His whole body was shaking. Later. Not now. He knew it couldn't be now, and yet he could picture it so clearly, lying on one of those flat rocks, her body spread out beneath him. His hands capturing hers, pressing down against the stone. Her hair would dry and turn to red-gold like leaves in autumn. He'd take his time. He'd explore every inch of her body with his mouth. She'd cry out. She'd make those little sounds in the back of her throat. The effort to stifle his pent-up desire made his chest ache. If he didn't know better, he'd think he was a candidate for heart surgery. Wanting her that much was pure torture. But if she wanted to wait, he'd wait. He'd do anything she wanted, including forgetting the whole thing.

Out of the forest came the sound of footsteps crashing through the brush. He raised his eyebrows and sent her an inquiring look. "Bear?" he asked as calmly as possible.

She cocked her head. "Moose. He's probably smelled us. He'll head the other way. Maybe we should head out of here, too," she said. "It seems ridiculous to put our wet clothes back on when I have those dry clothes on the boat." She sounded so matter-of-fact, he couldn't believe he'd understood her correctly.

"But…" Run back to the boat naked? He was dizzy from the picture in his mind, just thinking about watching her dashing down the trail. This time instead of focusing on the way her wet clothes clung to her skin, he'd focus on her firm, round, bare bottom. Did she know what she was saying? "You mean…"

"Yes, after all, you're a doctor, you've seen naked bodies before. Isn't that what you said?"

"Yes, sure, but—"

"If you're embarrassed about my seeing you…" she said, a glint of amusement in her eyes.

"Not at all," he said quickly. Embarrassed was not the word. He was only aware that when and if she saw him in the raw, she'd know just how much she turned him on. Just how ready he was.

"Then let's go." She turned and walked out of the pool. He closed his eyes, not out of modesty, but because she was so beautiful it hurt to look at her. Her whole body was glowing.

He opened his eyes and followed her to the rock where they picked up their clothes and carried them under their arms down the trail. He tried to act normal, but it was hard when his head was about ten feet above his body. He had this strange bird's-eye view of her and of himself walking along, stark naked. It was so improbable he was sure he must be dreaming.

She never glanced back at him. He didn't know why. Maybe she was shy or scared or embarrassed. She didn't act that way. She walked like a model with a book balanced on her head, straight and steady and as unselfconscious as if she did this every day. He tried not to stare at her. He tried to act as if he'd seen many naked bodies before. And he had. But that had nothing to do with her. Nothing to do with how he felt today. His whole body felt as if it had been wired and somebody had thrown the switch.

He walked behind her, just as he'd pictured, and he made conversation about the flora and fauna in a deceptively calm voice as he stared at her from behind. They talked about the abundance of moss, the spectacular ferns that lined the banks and the lichens underfoot. And all the time he wanted her more than ever. But he wondered if there would be a right time and a right place. He wondered if she'd just said later because she didn't want to say no. Maybe it would never happen. Maybe she didn't want it to happen. Maybe it shouldn't happen. For both their sakes.

When they got to the launch, she went inside the cabin and tossed him a pair of overalls, a shirt, some socks and rubber boots from the window. He dressed on the sandy spit of land. A few minutes later she came out of the cabin, dressed as he was in a similar outfit. She still didn't look at him. Her cheeks were pink. Maybe she'd just realized what she'd done, what *they'd* just done. More important, what they'd *almost* done. She looked off into the distance and motioned him aboard.

Before she started the motor, he put his hand on hers against the leather bench. He couldn't let the moment pass without saying something. Something to let her know how much it had meant to him. "That was incredible," he said. "Thank you for bringing me here."

She turned her head slowly and finally met his gaze, but just for a moment. She didn't ask the questions that hung in the air between them. What was incredible? Was it you? Was it me? Was it us together? He would have had to say, yes, yes, yes. He lifted his hand and tucked a strand of wet hair behind her ear. Her mouth curved slightly at one corner as if to acknowledge the intimate gesture, but she didn't say anything. She jammed the key in the ignition and they started back to town, toward civilization.

When they reached the dock in Mystic, a young girl was waiting for them. It was Allison who said her little brother had sprained his ankle playing basketball in the school gym and would the doctor come and look at it. "I heard you guys were out on the water. I was waiting here for you. Could you come too, Carrie?" she asked.

Carrie agreed, and after they'd moored her boat, they walked to the school together, the three of them. Matt asked Allison if she'd heard how Donny was.

"I was over there a little while ago. He looks better. His parents don't look so worried, either."

"I'll drop in on him as soon as I see your brother," Matt said. "I wish I had my bag with me. There's probably an Ace bandage in there. We'll need ice for his ankle.''

''Oh, we've got ice,'' Allison said with a smile. ''Plenty of ice.''

The high school was a collection of prefabricated buildings, the largest had been outfitted with a polished wood floor and turned into a multipurpose room with basketball hoops at each end and bleachers along one side.

Carrie was surprised to find it was dark inside. She stood in the doorway with Matt and Allison behind her. Suddenly the lights went on and the room was full of people holding balloons, smiling and yelling, ''Happy Birthday.''

Her knees wobbled, her face turned scarlet. She'd succeeded in putting her birthday out of her mind. It wasn't hard to do, given the emergency with Donny and the arrival of Matt. Carrie didn't like being the center of attention. She didn't like being caught in the spotlight. She glanced down at her baggy coveralls that smelled of diesel oil. If she had to have a surprise birthday party, couldn't someone at least have leaked the news to her? Couldn't she at least be wearing something decent? Apparently not. Here she was with the whole town looking at her and she looked awful, more like a drowned rat or a wet dog than the guest of honor at her own party.

She told herself not to be ridiculous. They'd seen her in much worse condition than that over the years. If she were being honest, she would admit that it was Matt she didn't want to see her in this outfit and this condition. She blushed even deeper knowing he'd just seen her with no clothes at all, au natural, wet hair....

Clothes or no clothes, she was relieved to have an excuse to avoid looking at him and talking to him for a while. Things had gotten so intense out there on the island. She should have known better than to take him to a hot spring. What did she think was going to happen? Did she think they'd get into the water completely dressed? Did she think there would be a couple of spare swimming suits in the boat?

Here in the multipurpose room, she had a duty to hug or be hugged by each and every member of the community and to be wished a happy birthday and to assure them that she really, really was surprised. She had to drink some punch, eat some birthday cake and wear a silly birthday hat.

"So you and the doc went out sight-seeing?" Russ, one of her father's old friends, asked after he'd wished her a happy birthday.

"Uh, yes. He's only here for a short time so I took him out to see the Russian church."

"Nice-looking young fella," Russ observed, watching Matt across the room through narrowed eyes. "How old are you today, Carrie, nearly thirty?"

"You hit it, Russ," Carrie said. "Exactly thirty."

"You know your dad always hoped you'd get married one day," he said. "Just in case he didn't mention it. Even asked me if I'd perform the ceremony since I'm the only one in town who's got the certificate from the state."

Carrie nodded. What could she say? I appreciate the thought, but if my dad wanted me to get married so badly, then he shouldn't have brought me up to live in a small town in the bush with two or three eligible men, and she used the term *eligible* loosely.

"This doc a single man?" he asked.

"Oh, no you don't," Carrie said, squeezing his arm. "No matchmaking allowed. I'm way too busy to think about getting married. What kind of husband would let me fly all over the state? I've noticed that most men want a wife who stays around, cooks and cleans, instead of running her own business."

"No one said you have to run your own business. You could sell it, you know."

"Sell the business?" She blinked. "Russ, you know how much it meant to my dad."

"'Course I do," he said. "It was his whole life. That doesn't mean it has to be yours."

"But it is." Carrie was shocked to hear the words come out of her father's friend's mouth. What on earth was he getting at? Wouldn't her father be spinning in his grave if he'd heard this conversation?

"Don't pay any attention to me," he said with a smile. "I just can't resist putting my two cents in. Doesn't mean I know anything. Just hate to see a pretty girl like you going to waste."

She stiffened.

"I like to think I'm accomplishing something," she said. "Not going to waste."

"Oh, sure you are," he said. "Whether you get married or not, you can keep working, you know. Lots of women do. There's got to be some men who aren't looking for a housekeeper. Nope, they'd be impressed at a woman who could run a business on her own. But that's just my opinion. The trick is to find those men. If you want one, that is. Maybe you don't. Maybe I should just keep my mouth shut," he said with a grin. He patted her on the shoulder and drifted off to talk to someone else.

Carrie stood alone for a moment in the middle of the crowd. The buzz of conversation continued around her. Helium balloons had floated to the ceiling. There was punch spilled on the floor and a dozen or so pieces of cake on small paper plates remained on a folding table next to the wall.

What was going on? She'd had some strange days in her life, but this was right up there with the weirdest. It was her birthday for starters. She'd forgotten about it, or had she just wanted to forget it? Turning thirty was a time to look back and ahead. Neither of which she was interested in doing. She found herself more interested in living in the moment.

Then there was the fact that she'd almost made love to a stranger today. She hadn't decided if she was sorry about it or not. Sorry she hadn't done it, or sorry she'd let things go so far. Next Russ suggested she should get married. He even said she didn't have to keep the business. Her father's business! All this time she thought she was indispensable up here. Now she found out there was one person who thought she ought to leave. Maybe there were others. That hurt. Of course, Russ never said she should marry an outsider exactly. Maybe he meant she ought to marry Stan. He wouldn't mind if she kept the business and kept flying. That way she could stay here, here where she belonged.

She looked around the room and counted exactly three bachelors in the right age group. One was Stan. One was Matt and one was George, who'd been hired on contract to build a sewage system. He was staying with the Pattersons. Her gaze shifted back to Matt. He was talking to Donny's father. They shook hands and the next thing she knew Matt was talking to Maggie. She felt a flash of jealousy so strong it felt like a dagger through her heart.

She looked away, and Allison came up to her and handed her a piece of cake.

"Thanks, Allison, I've already had one." Just the sight of the gooey chocolate frosting turned her stomach. She was not herself today. Far from it. She was not thinking straight. She felt like a jealous shrew.

"Were you surprised, Carrie?" the girl asked eagerly.

"I really was. I can't believe you pulled this off. This is the best surprise party I've ever had." She didn't mention it was the only surprise party she'd ever had, or that she wished she'd known about it in advance so she could have changed her clothes and combed her hair at least. "How did you do it?"

"Oh, it wasn't me. It was a whole bunch of people. I was just supposed to get you here. They were so afraid you wouldn't get back in time. But you did. Where'd you go, anyway, in that rain?"

"Just out to the Russian church." She decided not to mention the hot springs.

"How'd the doctor like it?" she asked.

"He thought it was great," Carrie said. "Most people don't know about the Russians being in Alaska."

"He's sure cute. That's what we think, the other girls and me. How old is he, anyway?" she asked.

"I'm not sure. Thirty-something, I think."

"Oh, that old," she said with a frown. "How old are you, Carrie?"

Carrie smiled. It was nice she didn't yet know you weren't supposed to ask adults how old they were.

"Thirty."

"Do you think he's cute?" she asked.

"Yes, I do," Carrie said, praying she wouldn't blush like a teenager and give anything away. "I'm even more impressed that he's such a good doctor and that he'd come all this way to help us out," she said primly. She couldn't have the teenagers speculating about her and Matt, too. If this continued the whole town would be talking about her and Matt long after he'd left. The arrival of a stranger was always good for gossip, but a stranger who looked like Matt and performed miracles would be fodder for the locals for months if not years. It was going to be hard enough to forget him, without everyone else reminding her.

"Too bad he can't stay. Sure would be nice to have a doctor in town. I mean, what if Jerry really had sprained his ankle?"

"I guess we could have handled that. But when anything serious happens, we have to get them out of here if we can or bring someone in."

"Did he know it was your birthday?" Allison said.

"Honestly, I'd forgotten myself. If you all hadn't given me this party…"

"Who would have made you a cake?" Allison asked.

"I guess I would have had to make myself one," Carrie said. A sudden, long-forgotten memory came rushing back of her mother making her a white cake with chocolate frosting, complaining about not finding birthday candles at the little local store. In a way it summed up her mother's experience in the bush.

Trying to cope, complaining, wanting things to be the way they were in California and always dealing with frustration.

Allison shook her head at the preposterous idea of making one's own birthday cake and went off to talk to her friends. Carrie told herself that she didn't care in the least that Matt was still talking to Maggie. She reminded herself he didn't know that many other people in town. After all, who did she expect him to talk to? It was a further sign of the friendliness of her village. She looked around and joined a small circle of old-timers who were reminiscing about the good-old days.

"There was the time your dad flew off to Sitka to buy pizzas for the whole basketball team when they won the district championship. What a guy."

Carrie smiled. Her father had left a legacy of good deeds and kindness behind him. She only hoped she could do the same.

When Matt came up behind her and put his hand on her shoulder, her knees buckled. She knew immediately who it was. She could smell the scent of rainwater and the wind and feel the heat from his body. His breath was warm on the back of her neck. She sucked in a sharp breath.

"I'm going to look in on Donny," he said.

"I'll come with you," she said.

"You can't leave your own party," he said. "Besides Maggie has invited me to see her collection of native jewelry."

"Oh." Inside the overheated gym, filled with at least fifty-something warm bodies, something inside her turned cold. "Fine. I'll see you later." What else could she say?

"I'll catch a ride back to your house," he said, and then he was gone. So was Maggie. She watched as they disappeared through the door with a sinking feeling in the pit of her stomach. What had she told Maggie? *I'm only interested in him as a doctor, nothing else.* She might as well have handed him to Maggie on a platter.

Of course, nobody could hand over another person. He had to want to be handed over. She was being ridiculous. Ordinary women had flirtations with men and didn't lose their heads over it. They went on with their lives, meeting other men, even having affairs. Why couldn't she? Because she wasn't an ordinary woman. She'd been raised by her father who taught her nothing about how to choose a man or handle one after you'd chosen him. He'd taught her many things like how to scare away a bear and how to repair a frozen plumbing pipe, how to predict the weather and how to fly a small plane. There were other things she should have learned on her own by now but hadn't. Like how to handle jealousy. How to say no when you wanted to say yes. How to be happy with what you had and not wish for more.

She'd never had even a discussion with anyone of how to act around men. How to judge a man. It was a mother's job to teach you how to choose a mate to spend the rest of your life with. How could her father teach her that when he'd bungled that decision himself. Because of her innocence and her naiveté, she'd made one major mistake. She was determined not to make another. She was glad Matt had gone off, because if he hadn't, she didn't know what would have happened next. She might have been tempted to make another major mistake. After that episode at the hot spring, she might have been more than tempted... But not now. Not anymore. Thanks to Maggie. Maggie was an attractive woman, and it was clear Matt was enjoying a rare vacation and a rare opportunity to do things he hadn't done before. Why shouldn't he take advantage of it to the fullest?

Chapter Six

Carrie stayed at the party as long as she could keep a smile on her face and manage to make some kind of conversation with the well-wishers. When most of them finally left, she helped clean up the gym, stuffing large plastic garbage bags with used paper plates, paper cups and plastic forks. It was good to have busy work to do, to keep her mind off Matt and Maggie.

Then she drove herself home, passing Donny's house and noticing that Maggie's station wagon was nowhere in sight. They'd be at her house by now. Her two-story house filled with comfortable Danish modern furniture she'd shipped up here when she married Bud. Right now they'd be sitting on her leather couch drinking brandy in front of her fireplace while she regaled him with stories of her adventures in the frozen North that certainly matched anything Carrie could tell and then some. Maggie would show him pictures of the time she raced her sled dogs across the Arctic with a previous boyfriend. Maggie could be very amusing and very sexy at the same time. She was never at a loss for men in her life. None of them seemed to stay very long, but that didn't seem to bother her. It shouldn't bother Carrie, either. She gripped the steering wheel so tightly her palms were sweating. She told herself to stop torturing herself. She told herself she'd brought this all on herself. She'd brought Matt here and she'd introduced him to Maggie.

When she got home she stoked up the fire in her woodstove and went upstairs to change her clothes. A glance in the full-length mirror in her bedroom confirmed what she'd feared. She looked like a wreck. She looked as if she'd been caught in the rain, and every bit of her thirty years. She could see the wrinkles at the corners of her eyes if she looked hard enough. Soon her hair would turn gray.

It was still red, but it had dried in frizzy curls from the hot steam at the springs, and the coveralls hung loosely on her body. Even though people in the bush seldom dressed up, even for a birthday party, everyone at the party had known about it in advance and had at least combed their hair and made an attempt to look their best. Everyone but her.

She couldn't help picturing Maggie. Maggie, who'd known about the party ahead of time and had had a chance to dress for it. She'd looked terrific in well-pressed wool pants and a black turtleneck sweater that set off her flawless complexion. Her blond hair gleamed in the overhead lights in the gym and Carrie wasn't sure, but it looked like she was wearing diamond studs in her ears instead of local jewelry. Maggie could have passed anywhere in the lower forty-eight for an attractive woman, and up here she really stood out among the folks who dressed for comfort and warmth instead of style. Carrie had always known that. She'd accepted the fact that Maggie was the town vamp. It was only now that it bothered her.

She vowed to upgrade her wardrobe the next time she was in Fairbanks or Anchorage. Not to catch a man. Just to feel better about herself. Right now she felt rotten about herself and pretty much everyone else. She kicked her rubber boots off and hit her toe on the closet door. She swore out loud, glad that she was alone in the house, where no one could hear her. It was a relief to get the boots off and it was a relief to swear and shout. In the absence of any nice clothes, or a facial or a manicure, the thing that would make her feel better about herself right now was a hot bath, a cup of hot chocolate and watching some mind-blotting program on television.

She would not think about Matt. She would not wonder when and if he was coming back tonight. He was a free agent. He didn't owe her anything. Just the reverse. She owed him.

She was in the tub when she heard someone at the front door. Her heart leaped to her throat. She knocked the soap into the water and couldn't pick it up. Every time she tried, it slipped out of her grasp. Before she could get up and out of the tub, she heard his voice.

"Carrie?"

"Upstairs," she yelled back.

She heard his footsteps on the stairs. "I'm in the tub," she said, sinking down into the water. There were goose bumps all over her skin, despite the fact that she was submerged in hot water.

He stood outside the bathroom door. "Haven't you had enough hot water for one day?" he asked.

"I guess not," she said. "Have you?"

There was a long silence. The words hovered in the air. She wanted to take them back. She wanted to sink down, down, down and let the water fill her ears so she wouldn't hear the silence anymore. The harmless remark didn't come out the way she meant it. Or did it?

"Is that an invitation?" he asked at last. His voice sent a shiver of apprehension through her.

"No, no," she protested. "Just a question. Don't answer it. I'll be right out." She grabbed the shampoo and rubbed it through her hair. Maybe she couldn't be as glamorous as Maggie, but she could smell like a woman instead of a sailor.

When she came downstairs in clean clothes and clean hair, he'd lighted the fire in the fireplace and was fanning the flames. She noticed he, too, had changed from the boat clothes she'd given him to some well-worn jeans of her father's and a knit shirt that fitted his lanky, well-toned body better than could have been expected. She swallowed hard thinking of how she knew about the muscles in his legs, the taut skin over his lower belly....

He straightened and stood looking at her for a long moment with an intensity that made her self-conscious. Was he picturing her in the old baggy coveralls? Or was he remembering how she looked with nothing on at all. Or was he comparing her to Maggie? She wiped her damp palms against the sides of her pants.

"How was Donny?" she asked.

"Pretty much the same. Not up to chess, I'm afraid. Too tired. But the family is great, keeping up his spirits."

Carrie nodded. She offered him something to eat. A grilled-cheese sandwich? He said no, thanks. Donny's family had insisted he share a bowl of stew with them. She didn't mention Maggie. She didn't want to. She didn't want him to. Still, she wondered…

She sat on the hearth to dry her hair, trying to pretend this was an ordinary night. But nothing had been ordinary since the moment she'd first laid eyes on him.

"Why didn't you tell me it was your birthday?" he asked, standing in the middle of the room with his hands stuffed in his pockets.

"I forgot."

"I don't believe that. I've never known a woman to forget her birthday."

"And you know lots of women," she said with a touch of sarcasm that was unlike her. But then jealousy and envy were likewise unlike her.

"No, I don't. But the ones I do know, take my mother, for instance. Weeks before her birthday she drops hints of what she wants. Then my father buys it for her. Of course they go out for an elaborate birthday dinner."

"And your fiancée? Does she get the royal treatment, as well?" Carrie was sorry the minute she'd said these words. They came out sounding bitter and jealous. She really wasn't either. But neither was she herself. These past few days had brought out the worst in her. She didn't know what had happened to her, but ever since she'd met Matt her whole life had turned upside down.

Raised to be self-sufficient, she'd suddenly become dependent on someone who would be gone soon, and then where would she be? Oh, not dependent on his money or anything as mundane as that. It was far more subtle, far more insidious. She'd become dependent on his very presence. The look in his eyes, the way he smiled, the line of his jaw, the width of his shoulders, the way his hands felt on her skin. The way he made her feel—feminine and desirable.

He was the type who might never be dependent on anybody. She knew he loved and respected his parents, and of course he had a girlfriend, but he seemed to be so engrossed in his work he'd had no time for anyone else in his life. So she had to stifle this urge to make him want her as much as she wanted him. That wasn't possible. Raised to despise vanity, she found herself wishing for new clothes. As if that would make a difference. Raised to fear nothing, she now feared being alone for the rest of her life. What on earth was wrong with her? When would she be back to normal?

"She's not my fiancée. I can't marry Mira. I thought maybe I could. But once we started the cruise, I knew it wouldn't work."

"I thought it was all arranged," Carrie said.

"Oh, it was. By our parents. But adults in their thirties make their own decisions. Or they should. Besides, Mira deserves better."

"Better than you, an M.D. with a brilliant career ahead of him? Now you're being modest."

"She deserves someone who'll love her. I don't,"

he said brusquely. "Speaking of Mira, I should call the ship. Have you any idea of when the weather will clear?"

He must be anxious to get out of here. Despite what had happened out there on the island, or maybe because of it, he was getting antsy. She knew the signs. She'd observed them in the past and was helpless to do anything about them. She'd seen her former fiancé look out the window, look up at the sky and pace the floor. She remembered her mother trying to cope by doing volunteer work and writing travel articles about Alaska, but never able to completely shut out the call of the outside world, and finally giving in to the inevitable.

"I checked it out," she said. "It could clear tomorrow. At least there's a possibility. I can't promise, but it looks good."

"That's too bad," he said.

"What?"

"One of Donny's little brothers invited me to go fishing tomorrow, and you, too. I'd hate to disappoint him and honestly, they didn't believe this, but I've never been fishing before."

"Never been fishing? I don't believe it, either. Don't they have rivers or lakes in California? What about the ocean?"

"All of the above," he said. "But if you want fish you buy it at the grocery store. You don't need to catch it yourself."

"But it isn't as fresh. And you don't get the thrill of hauling in a fish you've caught yourself," she said.

"That's why I want to go. I've always wanted to go fishing, but until now I had no one to take me.

You need someone to take you, to show you how, to bait your hook and take the fish off it.''

"Someone like your dad, maybe?"

"Yes, like your dad. But not my dad. My dad was always working. That's the life of the big-city plastic surgeon. If he wasn't on call, he was giving a paper at a conference or teaching a class. He's well-known in his field, and you don't get that way by spending your weekends fishing.''

"Does that mean you'll follow in his footsteps?" she asked.

"Professionally? Yes, that's the plan,'' Matt said. Sometimes he wondered whose plan it was exactly. His path was clear before him. For years he'd plowed ahead, moving from college to med school to rotations and now this. The breaks had been few and far between. There hadn't been time to think about the big picture. Until now. Until it was too late.

He reached in his back pocket and pulled out a small box. "I went to Maggie's to do some shopping for your birthday present,'' he said. "She said she had some jewelry for sale that you might like. She showed me her whole collection of native folk art and crafts and antique Russian artifacts and I saw how she sells her stuff on the Internet. She's certainly enterprising.''

"Yes, she is,'' Maggie murmured. "Enterprising and glamorous and a lot of fun, too.''

Her eyes widened in surprise when he put the box in her hand. What had she expected? Had no one given her a birthday present before? What about jewelry? Again his experience with women, like his mother and Mira, was that jewelry was an appropriate gift at any time. They appreciated it, they expected it and they treasured it. But Carrie was not like the other women in his life. Maybe he'd made the wrong decision.

"You didn't have to do that," she said, staring at the box.

"Open it," he said. "It won't bite. And if it doesn't fit, or you don't like it, I can take it back. When Maggie showed it to me, I thought it would be right for you."

"I'm sure it will be," she said, but she still didn't open the box. She sat there staring at it while her eyes filled with tears.

"What's wrong?" he asked, sitting down next to her and pulling her close, so close the smell of her shampoo and the soap on her skin made his pulse quicken. "Did I do something wrong?"

She shook her head. "It's just…I wasn't expecting anything." She tilted her face in his direction and let out a sigh. "Thank you."

"Maybe you'd better look at it before you thank me." Now he was really concerned it wouldn't be appropriate or she wouldn't like it. He wanted to give her something to remember him by. If she wanted to remember him. As for him, he needed nothing to remember her by. He knew he'd never forget these amazing days, and he wasn't ready to have them brought to a close. He'd determined to stay over tomorrow, no matter what happened with the weather.

Finally, after she sat there running her fingers over the box for an eternity, she opened it and looked inside at the ring made of silver set in an intricate, old-fashioned setting with an amber stone. Again, a long silence. He couldn't stand it any longer. He took it out of the box and slid it onto her finger.

"Say something, Carrie," he said. "Do you like it?"

"It's beautiful," she said, holding up her hand. "I-I've never had anything so beautiful. I don't know what to say."

He hadn't realized he'd been holding his breath until she was actually wearing the ring. He didn't know what to say, either. He'd been so afraid she'd think she shouldn't accept it. Or that she wouldn't like it. What a lucky break that he'd been able to buy her something so perfect in this outpost. Maggie had been so helpful. She'd instinctively known what would be right for Carrie. When he saw the gem, he knew it, too.

She twisted the ring around on her finger. "The setting is lovely. It looks old, is it Russian?"

"Yes, Maggie said most amber comes from the Baltic. The Russians brought it with them, to trade or just to wear. She's had this for a while in her collection. I couldn't have found anything I liked better. But the main thing is whether you like it."

"I do," Carrie said so softly he had to bend forward to hear her. Then she put her hand on Matt's cheek and kissed him. She meant it only to be a thank-you kiss and she thought he knew it. She was afraid of starting something she couldn't finish tonight and then he'd fly off tomorrow and she'd be left more alone than she'd ever been in her life. But how else to express what she was feeling, the gratitude, the tenderness, the affection, than by a kiss? But she was feeling more than that. Much more. She was bowled over by the thought that had gone into the gift. That he'd cared that much.

He didn't kiss her back, but he traced the outline of her mouth with his finger. There was a flutter in the area of her heart, but this time she didn't lose her head. She thought he was sincere about wanting to fish tomorrow, but if the weather cleared, he'd be out of there, gone forever, fishing or not. She had to preserve some shred of pride and discipline. As much as she wanted to make love to him, she was not going to. Not tonight. Not ever. She might be naive, self-deluded and impulsive, but she also had some sense of self-preservation.

There were questions in his gaze. She could only imagine what those might be. What about later? What about finishing what we started? What about what happened out there on the island?

She didn't have any answers so she didn't give him any. Instead she suggested he call the ship and give them an update on the weather conditions, as much as he could.

When she went to her room, she opened the window and looked up at the sky. She didn't know whether to hope for clear weather or not. Matt seemed to genuinely want to go fishing. And her? What did she genuinely want? She didn't dare answer that. She wanted what she'd always wanted. A man like her, who'd been raised in the bush, but educated outside. Who knew and understood both worlds but had chosen this one as she had. She'd tried to find such a man once, she thought she'd come close enough, but she'd been wrong. She wouldn't try again. It was too painful when they turned their back on her and her way of life and left.

She closed the window and went to bed with her ring on her finger, lying on her back with her eyes closed, lightly polishing the smooth surface of the amber with her fingers. It was the best present she'd ever gotten. The best birthday she'd ever had.

Again she overslept. Matt was knocking on her door, saying he was going fishing. She looked out the window. It was gray and cloudy. The weather hadn't changed.

"Wait," she said, opening her bedroom door. "I'll come with you."

"Sorry," he said. "I'm late already. I told Bradley I'd be there at eight. I have to buy some equipment at Merry's store first."

When his gaze slid over her nightgown and down to her bare feet, she felt like he was undressing her right there in the hallway. She took a deep breath and forced herself to think about fishing. "You don't have to buy anything. We must have some old poles in the shed," she said.

"I have to do this right," he said. "And get my own stuff. I may never have another chance."

"Where are you going to fish?" she asked. "I'll join you there later with a picnic lunch."

"Have you heard of a place called Willard's Pond?" he asked. "Where the trout jump out and beg you to catch them?"

She grinned at the tale she'd heard over and over but never believed. "Yes, of course. I'll meet you there. You take the truck, I'll hitch a ride."

"You're sure?"

"Positive. The keys are in it."

There was a long pause. He looked well rested and alert just like yesterday morning. Crisp dark hair. Firm jaw. Broad shoulders. Wide-awake-but-sexy, heavy-lidded eyes. She knew how she looked next to him, rumpled, sleepy, tousled. She could have stayed in her room. She should have. Then they could have had this conversation through the door. But no, she had to have a look at him.

He finally spoke. "I, uh, I decided it wasn't flying weather," he said. "I trust you agree?"

"You're probably right," she said. "I'll check it out."

He didn't wait for her to check it out. He turned and she heard his footsteps on the stairs, then the truck's engine and then he was gone. She smiled to herself thinking of how excited he'd looked. As if he was a kid going fishing for the first time. Arrested development. Was that what he said he had? She preferred to think of it as enthusiasm for what was new. She loved seeing her life and her town and her friends through his eyes. Even Maggie.

She took her time getting dressed, wearing some faded jeans that had shrunk and now fitted like a second skin and a coral-colored sweater that sent some color to her cheeks and made her hair look more mahogany than fiery. Why was she dressing so carefully for a fishing trip to a local pond? She wouldn't even consider the question. Maybe she was afraid she already knew the answer. Besides, she was much too busy making a picnic lunch with deviled eggs and tuna-salad sandwiches and frosted brownies.

When she was ready, she called Granger Hill who

lived farther out than she did and asked if he was going to town. He went to town every day so she wasn't too surprised to have him offer to pick her up. When he saw she had a large wicker picnic basket, he insisted on taking her straight to the pond.

"Heard you got yourself a boyfriend," he said before he let her off.

She felt her cheeks turn the color of her sweater. "No," she said, twisting the silver ring around on her finger. "That's not true, and I'll thank you to set the record straight if you get a chance. The man is a doctor who came here out of the goodness of his heart to see our Donny. He's staying with me, yes, but that's because I have a spare room and I'm the only one he knows. If I had a boyfriend, you'd be the first to know, Granger. That's just a rumor. You know how rumors get started in this town, don't you?"

"Yes, I sure do, Ace," Granger said with an amused glance at her, reminding her of the nickname her father had given her that had stuck for many years. "Of course I'll be glad to do that. Set the record straight, that is. No problem. Well, here we are now. That looks like your truck there. I can't drive you any farther. Think you can make it up the trail to the pond okay?"

"Of course. Thanks a lot." She stood watching him drive back down the one-lane dirt road and started up the path.

MATT LISTENED PATIENTLY while Bradley showed him once again how to bait his hook with one of the expensive flies he'd just bought. For some reason the flies always fell off or got eaten off before he ever caught a fish. Bradley and his friend already had a bucket full of good-size trout while Matt had none. Maybe it was because they were using inexpensive worms. It was especially galling because Matt had a brand-new pole, a selection of flies, a net and a fancy cooler to hold his catch, which so far was nonexistent.

He really didn't mind. He sat on a rock at the edge of the pond holding his new pole in his hand. The wind had died down. The trees were still, and redolent of pine. Gulls squawked and circled, looking for handouts. The two boys, Bradley and his friend Skip, dangled their lines in the water and talked about school and friends and things that boys talk about wherever they live. They were only serious when asking about Bradley's brother Donny. Matt assured them he was probably going to get well. There was no sense in scaring them for no reason. Telling them any details would only confuse them.

"You boys come here often?" he asked.

"My dad brings us sometimes, when he's not out logging," Bradley said. "My mom says it's his way of getting out of work around the house. But he says, 'Do you want some fish for dinner or not?' And you can't live in Alaska and not fish. What about California, Doc?" Bradley said. "You never went fishing down there?" The boy leaned forward and hauled in another fish. Matt shook his head in surprise as the boy expertly removed the hook from its mouth and plopped it into his bucket along with all the others.

He sounded just like Carrie. Amazed that he'd grown up without such an essential skill.

"Nobody ever took me," he said. "My dad was too busy. So I appreciate you guys helping me out here. What I don't understand is how you catch all these fish with a pole and a string and a worm on the end of your hook and I've got all this new equipment and these beautiful flies and nobody's biting.''

The boys laughed and offered to find him a long stick. But he laughed, too, at his own ineptitude and shook his head. If someone had told him he'd be spending a day doing nothing but sitting on a rock, holding a pole in his hand for hours, staring at the water under a leaden sky without being bored or worried about wasting time, he'd have said they were crazy. But here he was, enjoying the company of two eight-year-olds and doing absolutely nothing. Not a medical textbook in sight. Of course he was supposed to be catching fish, but they weren't cooperating with him today. Not that he cared. What he cared about was the impending arrival of Carrie.

While he waited, he wondered if he'd ever go fishing again. Would anyone ever take him fishing again, or more important, would he ever take anyone fishing with him? Would he ever have another break in his life like this, or would he turn out like his father, working until his heart gave out, and then in his sixties be forced to cut down on his practice and only then look around and realize what he'd missed and take a cruise to Alaska. The prospect wasn't appealing. But what was the alternative? There wasn't one. He loved medicine. He loved treating patients. He loved the challenge of making a diagnosis and then the satisfaction of seeing his patients get well.

He'd put in all these years and there was no going back now. He'd been given a few days of freedom and he would enjoy them. But there weren't likely to be many more like this.

Bradley laid his pole down and sat cross-legged next to Matt on the rock. "You're not married, are ya?" he asked. "That's what my mom said."

"That's right. I've been going to school for a long time. That's what you have to do to be a doctor. So I haven't had time to get married."

"Do you have a girlfriend?" Bradley's friend asked.

"Yes," Matt said reluctantly.

"It's Carrie, isn't it?" Skip asked.

Matt didn't know what to say. Fortunately, the boys didn't wait for his answer.

"You got one, too," Bradley said, pointing to Skip. "You like Jenny Bradshaw."

"I do not. She stinks."

"You do, too."

The boys splashed water on each other until Matt told them to stop. They switched their attention back to him.

"What about Carrie?" Skip asked.

"She's nice, very nice. I like her a lot."

"Does she like you?"

"I think so. I hope so. You could ask her when she comes with our lunch."

"See?" Skip said to his friend. "I told you."

"Hey, there she is."

Matt turned his head and saw her walking toward them with her picnic basket in her hand. Her cheeks were flushed from the walk up the trail and matched the color of her sweater. He stared at her as dazzled as he was the first time he'd seen her. How could it be like that? How could she make him feel as if there were rockets going off inside his chest every time he saw her? It couldn't last. Another day or two and he'd come off this high. He had to. Otherwise he'd never be able to leave. He'd never get back to normal. Never be able to study or work again.

He was already dreading the day the sun shone through those clouds above them. Every night he prayed for clouds. He prayed for rain or hail or even snow. It was hard to pray for clouds and then pretend to be disappointed when the skies didn't clear. So he'd stopped pretending. He'd admitted he was having a good time. No one could possibly know just how good a time he was having. Except for Carrie. He set his pole down and went to relieve her of the heavy basket.

"If I'd known when you were coming I would have met you down below and helped you with the lunch. This is the lunch, I hope," he said, raising the basket to gauge the weight. "My pals and I are starving."

"No, it's some extra bait I thought you might need," she said with a grin.

He shook his head. "I've got enough here to last for a year."

"Where did you get all that stuff?" she asked, taking in his spinning reel, his fly-casting pole and his tackle box, open to reveal a large selection of flies.

"From your friend Merry's store. She said this is what I'd need for trout fishing."

"Do you know how to cast?" she asked.

"No, but the boys are trying to teach me." He

waved to the boys who had wandered to the other side of the pond.

"How many have you caught?" she asked, looking in his brand-new cooler.

"Not a thing. In the meantime, the kids have been pulling them in one after another. Look there in their bucket. They use sticks and string and worms and fish eggs."

"That's the traditional method. Sounds like Merry saw a chance to unload a lot of gear on you," Carrie observed.

"I asked for it," he said. "I told her it was my first time. I said I wanted to do it right."

When the boys saw Carrie spreading her checkered tablecloth on the mossy ground, they came running. They chugged fruit juice from her thermos while she set thick sandwiches of tuna salad on sourdough bread on paper plates.

"This looks great," Matt said, sitting on the edge of the cloth and taking a deviled egg from the plastic box. "No wonder fishing's so popular up here if you get to have a lunch break like this."

"Do you think you deserve lunch after such an unproductive morning?"

"Unproductive? I'll have you know I've been thinking. I've never had so much time to think as I have since I came here."

"Time to think. That must explain why we're all so smart up here," she said.

He grinned and tossed a stick of celery at her. For a moment the boys looked shocked at this childlike behavior, then they burst into laughter and started crumpling napkins into balls to toss at each other.

"All right," Carrie said with a mock stern expression. "I don't suppose you boys want me to take my food and go home, do you?" By boys it was obvious she included Matt, too.

They all protested loudly and she continued to bring out food from her basket—carrot sticks, potato chips and sweet pickles.

They ate in contented silence for a long while. Matt's eyes were drawn to Carrie's hand and the finger that wore the ring he'd given her. He wondered if she would wear it after he was gone. He wondered if she'd ever think of him after he was gone.

"Hey, Carrie," Skip said. "You must like the doctor a lot to bring up this lunch for him."

"I brought it for you, too," she said, but Matt noticed a telltale flush spread to her cheeks.

"Yeah, but you do like him, don't you?" Bradley said. "'Cause he likes you."

"How do you know?" she asked, carefully avoiding Matt's gaze.

"He told us," Bradley said with a knowing grin.

"So you all were talking about me. What else did he say?" she asked, her eyes sparkling.

"He said he's in love with you," Bradley said, and then burst into helpless laughter at his audacity.

"He wants to marry you," Skip added, slapping his knees.

"Boys, boys," Matt said with mock severity. "I told you not to tell."

"So that's why men go fishing together, to talk about girls," Carrie said.

"Not just you," Matt said. "We were talking about Bradley's girlfriend. What's her name?"

"Jenny."

"Hmm." Carrie looked at Matt. "I thought you were up here thinking."

"You can only do so much thinking, especially without brain food. Now that I've had one of your tuna sandwiches, I think I can do some more."

"Here's something to think about," she said. "What are you going to do with all this equipment when you leave?"

"Can I leave it with you?"

"You can, but…are you sure you won't want it someday? Someday when you have a son or a daughter. I used to come here and fish with my dad."

"You're lucky he got to spend so much time with you," he said soberly. He wondered if his father had ever pondered the sacrifices he'd made to pursue his career. Not that Matt had suffered; he didn't remember ever feeling deprived. It was his dad he felt sorry for. For missing out on his only son's childhood.

"My dad wanted to make sure I would be self-sufficient. That I could catch my own fish and grow my own vegetables. I confess I've had many days like the one you're having, where everybody catches their quota and I get nothing."

"But you're successful where it counts, you fly your own plane," he said.

"Yes."

"I can't believe you could grow vegetables up here," Matt said.

The boys wrinkled their noses at the change of subject, helped themselves to the frosted brownies she'd brought and went to look for frogs on the other side of the pond.

"I'll have to show you my garden. Of course it's a short growing season, but it can be done. These pickles you're eating? I grew the cucumbers."

"You're a remarkable woman," he said.

"Because I grow cucumbers?"

He lay back on the matted moss and looked up at the sky. The gray sky that was keeping him here in Mystic.

"Not just because you grow cucumbers. You make pickles out of them. As if that wasn't enough, you're a pilot. You also blush at compliments. You forget your own birthday. You make delicious cinnamon rolls. I could go on." He sat up, reached across the tablecloth and took her hands in his. He rubbed the stone in the ring he'd given her with his fingers. "When I saw this ring I thought of your eyes. I thought they were exactly the same color." He held her hand up to her face. "I was right."

Carrie didn't know what to say. She'd never received such an exquisitely thoughtful present. But she didn't want to make more of it than she should. It was just a birthday present from a man who she'd never see again. A kind of thank-you present for her hospitality. It wouldn't do to become attached to either the ring or the man. Yes, she could keep the ring even after the man had gone, but maybe she wouldn't ever wear it again if it brought back too many memories. She was smart enough to know there was going to be a letdown after he left. She had to be prepared.

"I don't know what to say," she said. "Except thank you." To have an excuse to pull her hands back from his, she put away the plates and the leftovers from their picnic. "Will you be doing any more fishing?" she asked.

"Maybe not," he said. "Casting is much harder than I ever thought. Why don't you give me a demonstration."

"Wait a minute. I'm not sure I remember exactly how."

"Come on, you're a self-sufficient Alaska woman. I want to see you do it. You don't have to catch anything. Just cast."

He helped her fold the tablecloth, then they went down to the edge of the water. She picked up his pole and rested it on her shoulder.

"I don't know," she said. "I'm a little rusty at this, but it's something like this."

"Just a minute," he said, stepping behind her. He ran his hands along her shoulders. "Just to get the feel of it," he said. But the touch of his hands distracted her so much her mind went blank and her body refused to cooperate.

"Nope," she said lightly, swinging the pole back behind her and then letting the line drop. "I can't do it, either. Maybe you should just use the stick and string method the boys use."

"Is that what you're going to tell your kids?" he asked, leaving his hands on her shoulders. He brushed the back of her neck with his lips, and she had to set the pole down.

"Kids? I'm afraid it's getting a little late for kids," she said, as she realized what she said was only too true. A kind of sadness that she hadn't expected filled her heart. "Maybe I didn't tell you, but I turned thirty yesterday. Maybe that's why I didn't tell you or why

I forgot on purpose, so I wouldn't have to think about turning thirty.''

"It's not that old," he said, applying pressure to the back of her neck. "You're not too old to get married and have kids. You said you were engaged once. What happened, Carrie?''

"Did I? Did I say that?" she said. She was stalling for time. She'd intended to pack up and go home, but she didn't seem to have the energy or the inclination to leave this peaceful spot. Though she didn't want to talk about her failed plans for marriage and a family, maybe it was time she did. Maybe when you turned thirty, you couldn't avoid looking back and ahead whether you wanted to or not. She moved to the tablecloth, now cleared of the picnic items, and sat down on the edge of the cloth. She hugged her knees to her chest. Looking back was one thing, spilling your past to an almost stranger was another. She searched her mind for another topic, something else to talk about, to change the subject, but Matt was too quick for her.

"Who was he?" he prompted, as if he was afraid she was going to avoid his question. Though why he wanted to know, she didn't know.

"He was someone I met in college," she said, realizing she couldn't put it off any longer. "He was fascinated by my so-called exotic background." *Just like you are,* she thought, glancing at Matt who'd come over to sit on the ground, leaning against a rock with his feet out in front of him. "He just had to see it. He thought he'd love it up here. The last frontier, the open spaces, the clean air, the unspoiled land. No traffic, no noise. He wanted to be a writer. He thought this would be the perfect place to do it with no distractions. He was right, there were no distractions. That was the problem. He quickly found that he couldn't stand it. Not just the isolation, though that was part of it.

"He realized how much he needed a corner coffee bar to hang out in, a place to go to scribble on his notepads. He had to have a group of writers to meet with, to share the ups and downs of the creative life as he called it. But that wasn't all. Mystic seemed provincial. Of course it *is* provincial. I never said it was the Left Bank." She couldn't hide the bitterness in her voice. "But he made fun of the people, of my friends, my community. That hurt."

"You must have been disappointed," Matt said gently.

"Disappointed in my judgment," she admitted. "I should have known. Before that, my mother left for almost the same reason."

"She needed distractions, friends?"

"Something like that. Actually nobody really said what it was. My dad sure didn't want to talk about it. She always sent me a birthday present and he'd look at it without saying anything. He just had this look on his face. I imagined him saying to himself, *Fine, you send her a present. You think that's what it takes to be a parent? Think again.* Maybe he didn't say that. Even to himself. I don't know. Oh, that's why I forgot my birthday. No present from my mother because there's been no mail delivery."

"Have you seen her recently?"

"She came up for my dad's funeral. We didn't really talk. I don't know how she felt. Maybe she didn't, either. Probably regret and relief and sadness and who knows? I was too sad to make the effort to bridge the gap between us. She seemed like a stranger to me. I saw her look around the house, and I think she must have been relieved she'd left. I drove through town with her and I thought about how it must look to her. Probably the way it looks to any outsider. Small and shabby and weather-beaten.''

''Not your house. She couldn't possibly have thought that. Your house looks warm and welcoming and comforting.''

''You think so? Really?''

''I really think so. Surely your boyfriend could see that,'' he said.

''I guess so. But it wasn't enough. Not enough for my mother, not enough for Tony.''

''But enough for you?''

''Of course,'' she said a little too quickly. ''Or I wouldn't be here.''

''If you loved Tony, why didn't you live where he wanted to live, wherever that was.''

That was the big question she'd never wanted to answer. She didn't want to face the possibility that she'd made the wrong decision. She picked up a stick and drew a stick figure in the dirt and tried to justify her decision. Not to Matt, to herself.

Chapter Seven

She thought over her answer for a long time before she spoke. "Of course he suggested that I leave and go live with him in the lower forty-eight. But I always knew this was where I belonged. I was raised to take over for my dad. It would have broken his heart if I hadn't come back. Dad must have thought of the possibility of my staying down there somewhere, but he never said anything. We were going to be partners. Neither of us knew I'd be taking over for him so soon. Now that he's gone it's even more important for me to be here. Oh, the business is flying all over the state, but when somebody in town needs something or needs to go out I'm here for them." Surely he could see that, even after only a few days in town.

"Like the other day," he said.

"Yes. That was unusual. A real emergency. Mostly it's other things. Not so urgent. I love being needed and wanted. I love being a part of the town. A part of a community where I know everyone and they know me."

"I sensed that at your party. It was there in the air. This wonderful reciprocal feeling. They love you and you love them. That's very rare to have a whole town feel that way.''

''They felt that way about my dad, too. That's what I've inherited. That's what I can't give up.'' She glanced at him. She wondered if she'd talked too much. If she'd given away too much. If she'd sounded too judgmental. If she'd been too chauvinistic about her life and the town. She wondered if she'd bored him. He didn't look bored. He looked thoughtful. He looked as if he thought every word she said was important. He was a good listener. Just one of the characteristics of a good doctor. She had no doubt he'd be a good doctor—the best. Actually, he already was a good doctor.

''I'm envious,'' he said.

''Why? Isn't your situation similar...even better? Won't you inherit a whole list of patients you'll take over from your father along with a lot of love and goodwill? After all, he's done more for them than I'll ever do for anyone in Mystic. I can't give them a new face or repair any damage that will give them a new lease on life the way you can. *I'm* envious of you.''

He smiled at her. ''It's certainly true there's the possibility to do good work—important work,'' he said. ''But sometimes I wonder if I'm the right person to do it. There's a price to pay for spending all those years in school and in training for this specialty. And it doesn't stop there. I think I told you my dad was never around when I was a kid. He's still not around. The only reason he's on this cruise is because his doctor told him he had to take a break. His heart isn't strong. Whether that's because of his work or his disposition or his genes, we don't know. What we do know is that he's a workaholic. He loves what he does, and you're right, he is appreciated in return, not just by his patients, but by the whole medical community.''

"It sounds like a good life," she said.

"For him, it has been," he said. "So good he can't imagine anyone not wanting it."

"Like you?"

"Especially not me. I've been raised for it. Ever since I can remember that's what they've expected of me."

"No brothers or sisters?" she asked.

He shook his head. "I'd never raise an only child."

"It can be very lonely," she said. With a doting father, she'd often wished for someone to share her father's love. Sometimes it was too intense, one parent, one child. "I don't suppose your father has any idea you have any doubts?"

"Oh, no. It would break his heart if he thought I was even considering not taking over for him, which I'm not. Just as it would have your father's. There's no need to alarm him. I wouldn't seriously consider changing my mind any more than you'd consider doing something different."

"Have you talked to your parents on the ship lately?"

"No, I have to do that. I know they won't believe me, but I've been too busy fishing."

She looked pointedly at his empty cooler and smiled.

There was a distant rumble in the air. Her smile faded.

"What was that, thunder?" he asked.

''Sounded like it. We don't get many storms up here, mostly just steady rain or overcast. Let's go. I wouldn't want to get caught...'' She trailed off. No need to let him see how scared she was of thunder and lightning. It would make her seem like a wimp. She scanned the skies. No need to get scared, especially if it never came this way. But just in case...

''Come on, boys,'' she called across the pond. ''Time to go home.''

The boys carried her picnic basket between them, laughing as if they didn't have a care in the world as they charged down the path ahead of Matt and Carrie. They loaded the truck, and Carrie and Matt dropped the boys off at Bradley's. Then they went in to see how Donny was getting along. The living room was full of small kids watching a cartoon on TV, and Donny's room was full of his friends who were doing their best to entertain him with news and gossip. He looked tired, and Matt chased them out.

Carrie waited in the living room making conversation with the family while she waited for Matt to do a brief examination.

''It's a blessing for us to have the doctor around for all this time,'' Donny's mother told Carrie over the loud noise from the television set. ''He's given us more of his time than he should. And he's refused to take any payment for it. I suspect he needs to get back and get busy taking care of his own patients, don't you think?''

''Yes, but he says it's been a kind of vacation from his real work,'' Carrie explained. She didn't want Tillie to feel guilty about interrupting Matt's schedule or livelihood.

"I'm afraid he's not going to get out anytime soon," Tillie said. "I hear there's a storm coming in. A big one, this time."

"I thought I heard some thunder a while ago," Carrie said with a frown.

"Good you got your sight-seeing in yesterday. You don't want to be out on the water with thunder and lightning in the air."

"No," Carrie said. She didn't want to be anywhere except hiding under the covers with thunder and lightning in the air. That was only one of her worries. The other was rumors. Of course the whole town must know they'd gone to the Russian church, but did they also know they'd been to the hot spring? She hoped not. Rumors got started so fast up there and took on a life of their own. So far no one had said anything, but one never knew.

"Mom." Bradley suddenly jumped up from where he'd been sitting cross-legged on the worn carpet watching the movie on the small screen. He was wearing a big grin on his small face. "The doctor's staying here cuz he loves Carrie. He told us."

Carrie knew he was teasing. She knew she shouldn't react, but she felt her face turn red, anyway. She blushed just as easily now as she had when she was Bradley's age. When would she ever grow up?

"Bradley," his mother said sternly.

"It's okay," Carrie said. "He's kidding. He knows that it's impossible for somebody to fall in love in two days, don't you, Bradley?"

"Yeah, but the doc said he had a girlfriend."

What he didn't know was that the girlfriend was not her. She was somebody else. She was the kind of woman Matt would marry eventually. Maybe not now. Maybe not even her. But one of these days, he'd find someone like her and that would be it. The thought filled Carrie with a sense of fatalistic foreboding.

"Bradley, I don't think you've finished cleaning those fish you caught," his mother said. "You know the rules. Now get out there and get busy.

"It sure was nice of the doctor to take the boys fishing," Tillie said when her son had left the room.

"I think it was more the other way around," Carrie said. "They took him. And they caught all the fish."

"We'll be sure you have some to take home."

They had plenty to take home, all cleaned by Bradley and ready to cook. After Matt came out of Donny's room and gave his mother an update on his condition, he and Carrie drove back to her house. Back in Carrie's kitchen they put the cooler filled with fish on the floor.

"Next time maybe they'll be fish I caught myself."

She didn't say there wouldn't be a next time, but she thought it. No matter what he said, he knew it, too. His kind of lifestyle didn't permit long lazy days spent fishing. It hadn't up till now, and it probably wouldn't in the future. Enough of that. She had to warn him about the storm.

"I guess it's time I called the ship," he said. He sounded reluctant. It must be hard for him to keep explaining. "The cruise is almost over. They dock the day after tomorrow. Then they'll fly home to San Francisco."

"Oh, no." She leaned back against the kitchen counter. "You've missed out on so much."

"Don't say that," he said, crossing the room and placing his hands on her shoulders. "You have no idea how much this has meant to me." He framed her face in his hands and smoothed the worried frown from her forehead with the pads of his thumbs. She knew that was the doctor in him coming out. He had an innate wish to soothe, to heal, to take care of, not just her but everyone.

"I wish you could see this place through my eyes," he continued. "You're so used to it and the people and the water and the islands, you don't know how special it is. It's like nothing I've ever seen before. And you, you're the most special of all. You're like nobody I've ever met before. You've done so much for me. Made me feel so welcome. I want to recip-rocate. I want you to visit me and let me show you around my city the way you've shown me. I want to—"

"No, no, don't say it, you know you can't do that," she said, putting her fingers against his lips. "You know it's not possible. You've got a busy schedule ahead of you. You can't...I can't..." She couldn't finish her sentence. Why did she need to? He knew as well as she did it was impossible. She hadn't been out of Alaska for the past two years. Her life was here. Her job was here. Even if she did go, when would he have time for her? He wouldn't. It was just wishful thinking.

He didn't say anything else, but the intensity of his words and of his gaze convinced her he was sincere. Of course he was, but that didn't mean it was going to happen. Yes, he wanted her to come. But could she even imagine going to San Francisco, staying with him and having him show her around? Hardly. It made no sense at all. It would only make it harder for her to accept the inevitable—their paths would never cross again no matter how much she wanted them to. No, it couldn't possibly work out. Not in the long run. So why postpone the final goodbyes? Why make it more difficult than it already was to say goodbye? Why make her want something that would never happen?

She wished he'd never mentioned it. Because now she couldn't stop thinking about it. Her mind was full of images. She and Matt wandering up and down the hills of the city hand in hand. Though she'd never been there, she could see herself and Matt at Fisherman's Wharf eating cracked crab. The two of them on a cable car... She shook her head to erase the images.

He knew and she knew he couldn't drop everything to play tourist with her. Even worse she knew she wouldn't fit in. She could only imagine the looks his parents would give her. How disappointed they'd be to find he was interested in a bush pilot who was more at home in a cockpit than a hospital charity ball.

"No," she said. "I appreciate the thought, but it wouldn't work at all. You're busy, I'm busy. Neither of our schedules would allow anything like that." She ducked out from under his arms. "Go make your call. I'm going to fix some vegetables to go with the fish."

Matt stood in the doorway, reluctant to leave the kitchen. She'd made a fire in the cast-iron cookstove, which filled the room with a radiant heat. Her cheeks were flushed, her hair was tied back in a band, but tendrils had escaped and tempted him to wrap his fingers around them. But that wouldn't be enough. He'd want to wrap his arms around her, pin her against the whitewashed wall and kiss her until she was senseless. Until she returned his kisses, until she told him she was going to miss him as much as he would miss her. Until she said she'd come to see him. That she believed he would make it happen. That she'd do whatever it took to join him there. He told himself he was the one who was senseless. If he didn't come to his senses soon he didn't know what would happen.

He went into the living room and sat on the couch with his head in his hands. The idea of her coming to San Francisco had just popped into his head. It would make it much easier to leave here if he knew he could see her again. What if she brought Donny in? Of course she couldn't fly all that way in her little plane with him. And he'd have to be brought in on a gurney, but damn it, there had to be a way. But only if she wanted to come. So far she hadn't said she did.

If she came he'd find a way to take the time off. He'd never done it before. Never had a good reason. He refused to consider the fact that residents worked twenty-four-hour shifts and never had more than a day off at a time. He wouldn't consider the idea that her schedule wouldn't permit it or that she'd just say no. He'd find a way.

If not, tonight might be their last night together. If he never saw her again, he'd regret it forever if he didn't make love to her. He wouldn't suggest it. It would just have to happen. She'd have to give him a sign, or he'd feel like a fool starting something she didn't want to finish.

He didn't know when this idyll in this remote corner of the world would end. It could be tomorrow or it could be the next day. He wanted to take advantage of every minute. He knew he'd be sorry if he didn't. For a long time he sat on the couch with the phone next to him looking out the window. Far away he could see faint splashes of lightning flash across the sky. Again he felt guilty that he was enjoying the company, the simple pastimes, the scenery and the dramatic weather while his parents and Mira thought he was performing a great sacrifice. He smiled wryly to himself. If they only knew. If they knew they'd be upset, maybe even angry.

He sat back and watched the sky light up, and he relished the thought that he'd gotten another reprieve. Another day in paradise with Carrie. Paradise? No one on the ship would have called it that. He wasn't lying when he told Carrie the other tourists would have been delighted to see Alaska from the inside with an insider. But after a day or two, they'd be ready to return to the luxury of gourmet meals served by waiters in black-tie. As for him, he was looking forward to eating fresh fish cooked on an old-fashioned stove and as many more days like this that he could get.

He made himself pick up the phone and dial the number of the ship. He got through to Mira's room and she was there.

''Matt, what's happened? We've been so worried. We tried calling you but no one answered.''

''I'm fine. My patient up here is in stable condition. The reason I'm not back yet is because of the weather.''

"That's what you said the last time."

"This kind of overcast seems to last for days sometimes. This is one of those times. There's no possibility of flying out in a small plane and there are no large ones in this area. It's quite remote."

"That's terrible," she said.

"Yes, it is." What else could he say? No, it isn't terrible at all? I'm having the best time of my life? I don't want to come back? "Tell me, how was Ketchikan?"

"It was fine. Your father wrote postcards and your mother and I went shopping. They have the most marvelous stores. Of course they're packed with tourists from all the cruise ships, but we managed to do all our Christmas shopping and avoid the crowds later. We met the nicest people from Seattle who know your uncle Bob. Last night was the chef's night. The whole staff parades out of the kitchen carrying flaming baked Alaska. It's quite spectacular. I'm so sorry you missed it."

The smell of fish frying came wafting from the kitchen. Matt hadn't realized how hungry he was.

"I'm going to have to hang up now, Mira," he said. "It was good talking to you."

"Wait a minute," she said. "We'll be back in San Francisco tomorrow. When will you get home? How will you get back?"

"I don't know," he said. "I'll be in touch." He hung up and hurried into the kitchen in time to see Carrie flip several fish filets in her frying pan at once.

"Bravo," he said, raising his hands in the air and clapping. "That deserves a standing ovation. Tell me what I can do."

"Set the table, if you would," she said.

The kitchen was so small he brushed against her shoulder or her arm or her back every time he passed with the silverware or reached for the glasses or the napkins. The air was filled with steam from the pot of boiling green beans, and the tension was mounting. This amount of physical contact just wasn't enough. Not for him. After dinner, he told himself. Be patient. Watch for a sign. If she feels the way you do, she'll send a signal.

The fish was delicious. The whole dinner was wonderful. Then again, sitting across the table from Carrie eating bread and water would be wonderful, too. His knees bumped hers, once, twice and finally they came to rest against each other. She looked up at him, questions in her eyes, then looked away before he could answer them.

"This is the best fish I've ever had," he said.

"Because it's fresh," she said.

"Because you cooked it," he said.

She smiled and he saw the dimple flash once again. He stared, hoping to see it again. But she was in a serious mood.

"Did you get through to the ship?" she asked.

"Yes, they'll be going home tomorrow."

"You've missed most of the cruise."

"Yep."

She studied his face, no doubt surprised at his casual tone.

"I don't think they really missed me all that much," he said, realizing it was not just wishful thinking, it was true. He would have been a drag while they went shopping or postcard writing. "They wondered how and when I'm getting back. I said I didn't know."

"As to how," she said, setting her fork down. "I can fly you wherever you want, to Juneau or Fairbanks. You could catch a flight back to San Francisco. But when, I don't know. It all depends…"

"On the weather. Yes, I told them that. We have no control over the weather."

"I don't mind the rain," she said. "But thunder and lightning are another matter. I turned on the radio while you were on the phone. The weather report is for a big storm tonight." She looked out the window and shivered despite the warmth of the stove.

He gave her a quick look and saw her bite her lip. She'd hardly touched her food. "You're not really afraid of thunderstorms, are you?" he asked. "You've faced bears and flown through wind and rain and…I can only imagine what else up here."

"I know, I know, but…" She didn't finish her sentence.

"We hardly ever get this kind of electrical storm in California. Let's go in the living room and watch it out of your picture window."

"Uh…you go. I'll clear the table and do the dishes."

"And have you miss out on the pyrotechnics? No way. We'll do the dishes together."

She nodded, but she didn't look happy about it. She washed and he dried. A dish slipped out of her hands and crashed to the floor where it broke into a dozen pieces.

"Damn," she said softly. She stood and watched while he bent down, picked up the pieces and tossed them in the trash. Then she accidentally sprayed rinse water from the faucet onto her sweater. He took his towel and blotted the water off the swell of her breast. She drew in a quick breath and steadied herself with a hand on the rim of the sink. She looked at him with heavy-lidded eyes. She licked her lips and opened her mouth to say something but nothing came out. She might have been going to protest. He hoped not.

He wanted to trail his hand over her damp sweater, and draw circles around the outline of her breasts. He wanted to do more than make her gasp. He wanted to make her moan and cry out and give in to the pressure that was building and heading toward a climax that he knew was just as inevitable as the storm was. But he didn't do anything else except to dry dishes and exchange long, lingering glances with her when she handed him a wet glass or dish.

He was glad he wasn't the only one affected by the tension that was building between them. It was in the air and he knew she must feel it, too. His whole body was throbbing with the need to make love to her. But not unless she wanted it. Not only wanted it, needed it as much as he did....

Finally looks weren't enough. He brushed her arm with his hand when he took a plate from the sink. When she turned to face him, he reached out and touched her cheek with his finger. She held perfectly still, her gaze locked with his for a long moment before she turned back to the sink. He was waiting, as patiently as he could, looking for an opportunity to hold her in his arms, to kiss her in that tender spot behind her ear or to slide his hands under her sweater.

He was trying to be patient, to look for that sign he'd been waiting for.

When she'd finished washing the last dish, she took the towel out of his hands. "I don't really want to watch the storm come in," she said. "I want to bury my head under a pillow and try to pretend it isn't there."

"How about burying your head on my shoulder?" he suggested, pulling her against him. "Come on." He put his arm around her and gently dragged her into the living room to the couch. Outside the window, the lightning lit up the sky. It was a spectacular sight. She gasped and really did bury her face against his shoulder. He held her tight.

"I can't believe this," he said. "This is better than Fourth of July. Front-row seats for a spectacular show. I've never seen anything like this. Are you sure you don't want to have a look?"

"Positive." Her voice was muffled against his shirt. "I hate these storms. I think I'll go up to bed."

"And leave me here alone? You can't do that. I might get scared, too."

He could feel her lips curve against his arm. Despite her fears, he'd finally coaxed a smile out of her. He kissed the top of her head and buried his face in her hair. The scent of flowers filled his senses. She snuggled closer to him. With every roll of thunder he held her tighter. He angled his face to kiss her. She put her arms around his neck and kissed him back. Her eyes were shut tight. She trembled in his arms. Was that because of the storm or the kiss?

He didn't want to take advantage of her fears. He was trying to make her forget them. That was why he pulled her into his lap and nibbled at her lips, coaxing her to return his kisses. To distract her. He thought it was working. The louder the thunder, the brighter the lightning, the harder he tried to make her forget the storm. He wanted her to forget everything but him.

There was a giant flash of lightning that seemed to be right outside the house. The thunder followed in seconds with a giant crash. The lights went out. She shuddered and looked up at him with wide, terrified eyes. Her pale face was illuminated by the flashes outside. He got up from the couch with her in his arms, shifting her weight so she was pressed against him.

"Okay, that's it," he murmured, his lips pressed against her ear. "I see your point. It's time to hide under the covers." She could hide from the storm, but not from him. He'd spent two restless, frustrating nights under her roof, thinking about her, fantasizing about her and he didn't intend to spend another. He'd seen her naked body and he'd kept his distance, well, pretty much. He knew she wanted him. He could see it in her eyes, feel it when he touched her. But if she didn't want him tonight, he'd give her a chance to say so. Just so she knew it was now or never. Otherwise...

She didn't speak. She clung to him, one arm around him as tight as a vise, the other hand holding handfuls of his shirt in her fist. He carried her up the stairs two at a time, his heart beating double time, and stepped into her bedroom. For all the noise and the fireworks outside, there was still no rain hitting her windows. Not yet. Her room smelled of fresh air and the perfume that would always remind him of her. He set her on the edge of her bed. She leaned back and looked up at him, her eyes wide and unfocused.

"Don't look at me like that," he warned, "unless…"

"Unless what?"

Carrie was scared. Scared of the thunder, scared of the lightning. But more scared that he would leave her. She didn't want to be alone tonight. Not even under the covers. She wanted to be with Matt. It wasn't only the storm, it was more than that. How much more she didn't want to think about. This was not the time to think. It was the time to act.

She held out her arms. "Don't go," she said. "Stay here with me."

"Do you know what you're saying?" he asked. His eyes glowed. The desire she saw there was as hot as the lightning outside. She didn't want to talk about it anymore. She didn't want to discuss their impossible situation or whether this was right or wrong. She didn't want to argue the fact that they had no future together. That was a given.

She didn't care anymore. She didn't care that he would eventually marry someone suitable and she would never marry anyone at all. All the more reason to have one night to remember. She longed for him. She ached for him. He knew it. She was no good at hiding her feelings. She'd had no training. He was giving her one last chance to say no.

A huge flash lit the sky, and the boom that accompanied it set her heart racing. Something cracked like a gunshot then there was a sickening crash outside the house.

"That was too close," she said. Her lips were so

stiff they felt as if they were frozen. She ran to the window. The tree that had been in front of the house since her dad had built the place, was split in two and was lying on the ground. She gave a shudder that went through her whole body. Nothing was permanent. Everything was subject to nature. If she hadn't learned that by now, she'd better do it soon. She turned her back on the tree and the storm and went to the bed. He'd asked her a question. The words still hung in the air. More important than a fallen tree. More urgent than a power failure.

Did she know what she was saying?

"Yes," she said. She knew. The tree that had been struck by lightning was instantly forgotten. Her doubts and fears were gone. "Yes, yes, yes." She yanked at her sweater, but he was there before she could get it off, his warm hands tugging and pulling until he'd tossed it aside. Then he unhooked her white lace bra with such care and tenderness, it brought tears to her eyes. The bra had been at the bottom of her drawer until today, waiting…just as she'd been waiting, for someone to take it off and toss it aside. Why had she worn it? Who had she thought would see it? Today of all days. Pointless questions.

She wriggled out of her pants, and then all that was left was her white cotton bikinis. How ridiculous to worry about the last shred of clothes when he'd seen her without a stitch on. She'd seen him, too, and now she wanted to see him again. She wanted to touch the hard planes of his body. Her fingers itched to run them over his taut belly. She wanted to trail her lips from his mouth all the way down to his feet. To taste every inch of him. Just once. Then she could let him go. Then she'd at least have the memories. And no regrets.

First he had to take off those clothes. He stood and unbuttoned his shirt, then unzipped his pants. He wasn't wearing any underwear. He stood outlined against the window. Lightning flashed, and his beautiful body turned silver. She was suddenly more scared than she'd ever been. Scared he'd be disappointed. Scared she wouldn't know what to do. Scared he'd find her wanting.

She lay there and looked at him, her skin covered with goose bumps. She wanted him so badly. She wanted his arms around her, wanted him to end the suspense, to break the tension, to do what she'd been thinking about since the first time she'd seen him. If he was disappointed, if he was let down, so be it. It was too late to change her mind now. She thought she'd be embarrassed to see him fully aroused, leaving no doubt about what was going to happen, but she wasn't. She'd been waiting for this moment and now it was here. It was way too late for second thoughts.

He crossed the room, braced one knee on the edge of her bed, and looked down at her with hooded eyes. "Do you know how much I want you, Carrie? How much I've wanted you since I first saw you land your plane next to the ship and I saw you with your hair the color of autumn leaves and your jumpsuit that couldn't conceal your gorgeous body? Do you know how hard it is to sleep downstairs when I know you're up here lying in your bed?"

She hoped he didn't expect her to answer those questions because she couldn't speak. Her throat was clogged with emotion. Her eyes filled with helpless tears and she reached for his face and brought it down to hers. She kissed him on the mouth, and his tongue found hers and mated with it just as surely as they were going to mate tonight. She felt her whole body tremble as his tongue found the recesses of her mouth to explore and excite and tantalize.

At last. She wrapped her arms around him, and he crushed her breasts against his chest. She loved the feel of his body, heavy and hot, soothing, caressing, warming her, making her almost forget the storm outside. Just knowing how much he wanted her made her feel reckless, sexy, wanton.

She knew the storm hadn't stopped. She was vaguely aware of the booming thunder and the brilliant lightning, but they were only a backdrop to the drama inside her room. He loosened his tight hold on her and gently rolled her over on her side and looked into her eyes. Suddenly lightning lit the room again, and for a second she could see the passion in his gaze. She didn't know what he saw on her face, but he gave a small smile of satisfaction. Did he know, did it show that there was an ache deep in that secret place in her body that wouldn't be satisfied until he'd made love to her—totally, completely? Did he know how the pressure was building, higher and higher until she didn't know how much longer she could stand it?

Still, he took his time. He gazed at her breasts, just the heat from his gaze caused her nipples to bud and to peak. What would happen if… He took them one at a time in his broad surgeon's hands, to stroke, to touch, to caress. She thought she might faint from the sheer ecstasy.

"Yes," she murmured. "Yes."

"You are so beautiful," he murmured, "so incredibly responsive. I can't believe this is happening."

She tried to say something else, but her mouth was too dry. She arched her back and stifled a cry of pleasure. He held her by the shoulders and let his tongue take over from his skillful fingers, tasting, tempting, driving her almost to the brink.

"Please, Matt," she said in a strangled voice she didn't recognize as her own.

"Not yet," he muttered, trailing kisses down her rib cage and then over her gently rounded belly. He put his hands on her hips and his lips found the core of her being, the center of her body, the place no one had ever found before. She was stunned by the sensations that hit her. She cried out, begging him to stop or start or do something. She wasn't sure what.

He was sure. Sure of himself and sure of her. With a few strokes of his tongue, he awoke in her what he knew was there—passion and fire. She was hit by rolling waves of ecstasy, by an explosion that was stronger than any thunder or lightning storm.

She let the sensations roll over her, stronger and stronger—building and building until they crashed like the thunder outside the window. Her body convulsed. She lost all sense of time and place. The only thing she knew was that Matt was holding her tightly, murmuring words of endearment and desire. He cradled her head with his hands, covering her face with kisses until she stopped trembling. Her breathing slowed and she was filled with an incredible sense of fulfillment and wonder. So this is what it was supposed to be like.

She couldn't move, couldn't think, could barely breathe. He lay next to her, with her hand in his. She forced her eyes open. There was a smile of satisfaction on his face, but a second glance at his body reminded her he hadn't been satisfied at all. She leaned over him and looked into his dark eyes.

"Are you ready?" she asked. Silly question. If she didn't know he was ready by now, she needed a few anatomy lessons. She rolled over and straddled him, planting one knee on either side of his chest.

His eyes widened, his lips parted. "What do you think you're doing?"

"Giving you a taste of your own medicine," she said. Taste being the operative word. She wanted to taste every bit of him. She wanted to drive him just as crazy as he had her. She wanted to hear him beg for relief. She deliberately brushed the tips of her breasts against the hair on his chest.

He drew a ragged breath. He reached for her wrists and circled them with his fingers. "Let's get on with this." His voice sounded strangled.

"Oh, no," she said. "I'm just getting started."

"Then start," he said, his jaw clenched.

Suddenly she was shy. He'd called her bluff and now she had to show him how much she wanted him…how much she wanted him to hit the same heights she had. But what if she couldn't? She'd had so little experience.

She ran her tongue over his lips, nibbling and tasting. Just that. But that was enough to have him groan deep in his throat.

"Come on, Carrie," he said.

She moved on, ignoring his plea, warming to her

task. Rubbing her face over the hair on his chest, running her lips over the flat nipples. Noticing that he shuddered with ecstasy, but paying no attention to his pleas for more or less or something else entirely. When she got to his taut belly and his arousal, she looked up and met his gaze. In the darkened room, she felt rather than saw the heat, enough heat to scorch her hand as she let her fingers slide over the velvet shaft.

Before she knew what was happening, he was on top of her, and she was pinned to the bed. His hands were all over her, gently spreading her thighs, making room for him. As he entered her she heard her own voice cry out from somewhere outside her body. Before she'd had a chance to get used to him inside her, he pulled away. Then came in again. Slowly. Too slowly. Her body was on fire again. Wanting him. Now more than ever.

''Yes,'' she murmured. Though he hadn't asked a question. She was about to ask for more when he gave it to her. He came into her harder and faster, rocking her with sensations even stronger than before. When she hit the top of the arc and felt the room spin around and she heard him call her name, she knew there would never be another moment like this. She felt him lose the control he was clinging to and shudder with the same sensations that hit her. It was thunder and lightning without the fear. It was Fourth of July without the parade. It was Christmas and her birthday all rolled into one. It was the best present she'd ever gotten.

She lay there with his body on top of her, relishing the weight of him and the warmth of him. He rolled off and pulled her into his arms. She couldn't meet his gaze. A wave of shyness hit her. Had she been too bold? Had she come on too strong? The last few minutes—or was it hours?—had changed her forever. If it hadn't changed him, she didn't want to know about it.

She opened her eyes and peeked over his shoulder at the window. The storm continued. The room was dark, but every few minutes the thunder would boom and the lightning would light up the room. Not only the room but the whole world. Lying there in his arms made the storm recede into the background of the most amazing night of her life. A few hours ago it had been terrifying. Only a few hours? More than that. More like a lifetime.

Chapter Eight

"Tell me about it," he said after a long silence.

"It was incredible," she said, forgetting she was not going to go out on a limb until he'd said something first. What if he had sex like this all the time? Despite his busy schedule, what if he found time for sex between operations? She'd seen TV hospital dramas. She had an idea of what it was like. A quick embrace in the darkened examining room, a stolen kiss in the pharmacy or at the nurse's station.

"That's all?" he asked, grinning at her.

She blushed and hid her face against his chest.

"I would say it was a miracle," he said soberly, tucking a damp curl behind her ear. "But that's not what I meant. I want to know why you're so afraid of storms. You must have been through them before."

She rolled away from him and lay on her back. He pulled the sheet and her comforter up over them both.

"It's a long story," she said.

He propped his elbow next to her and braced his chin on the palm of his hand. His gaze was warm and steady. "I'm not going anywhere."

She bit her tongue to keep from contradicting him.

He *was* going somewhere. Oh, not now. Maybe not even tomorrow. But he was going and she was staying here. Still she owed him an explanation. Even if she didn't, she wanted to tell him about it. Maybe it would help. Not him, but her. Maybe she needed to go over it in her mind.

"It was a few years ago," she said, staring at the ceiling, tracing the familiar cracks with her eyes, thinking of all the years she'd slept in this bed alone. Knowing it would never be the same again after tonight. All those years she'd wished for someone to come along and make her life complete. All the while knowing full well no one could do that for you. You had to make your own life complete, understand yourself, love yourself before you could love anyone else. Maybe that was why she had to tell him. Not because he would understand her better, but because she might understand herself better.

She took a deep breath. "It was a few years ago. I was back from college, pretty much a full partner with dad, sharing the flight schedule. I was flying from Nome to Kotzebue, which is on the Chukchi Sea, when a storm came up. I had a load of king crab for a local festival as well as some spare parts for a garage. When I left Nome it was clear, and I heard nothing about any bad weather ahead. But a half hour or so out of town, I was on the radio and heard that a storm had come up just ahead of me. The control people in Kotz directed me around it. But before I could change course I was passing between clouds that were charged with electricity."

"What did it look like?" he asked.

"Sharp, bright zigzags." She shuddered, remembering how scared she'd been, how her teeth had chattered. "I thought I'd be okay as long as the clouds were above or below me, but I was wrong. The plane is metal, as you know. It makes a great conductor of electricity. I heard a loud boom that almost blew my ears out. I can't imagine a dynamite explosion could be any louder. It was white-hot and the whole sky was brighter than the brightest light. I was instantly and completely blinded by the flash. I couldn't see a thing. The lightning had jumped from one cloud to the plane and then hit the next cloud with me in between. All before I realized what was happening."

"You must have been terrified." He took her hand in his and gently stroked her fingers.

She nodded. "Terrified I was going to crash. Terrified I'd never see again even if I lived through it, because I was totally blind. All my instruments were blown out. I knew that, even though I couldn't see. I'd lost radio contact, of course. No way to call my dad and say goodbye or tell him how much I loved him. All those thoughts go through your mind."

Matt brought her fingers to his lips and kissed them. Just the touch of his lips on her skin made her pulse race and made her forget the past and the future. She forced herself back in time. She made herself concentrate.

"I kept thinking of what my dad used to say. 'Stay calm. Don't panic. You're a good pilot. You can get out of this.' Yes, I'd flown without instruments before. I could do that. But without my eyesight? Honestly, I didn't think so. I knew I had to keep the plane level, but how did I know what level was when I couldn't see the horizon?"

"How did you?" he asked, bending down to look in her eyes. His forehead was creased with worry lines, as if he didn't know if she'd gotten out of it alive.

"I didn't. I went into a dive, but I didn't know it. Not until I broke out of the clouds and my vision cleared. That's when I really started to panic. I was going down, down into the snow and the ice of the Arctic Circle.

"If I hadn't seen a half-frozen river outside a little village I wouldn't be here today," she said solemnly. "There was just enough water for me to land in. I made it down by the grace of God."

"And your skill as a pilot," he reminded her.

"Maybe. Anyway, when I landed the whole village came out. They'd heard from the radio tower in Nome that I was lost somewhere in the vicinity. I'm afraid I burst into tears when I got out of the plane and my knees collapsed. Especially when I saw my rudder was partially blown off. I would have crashed if I'd kept flying."

"How did you get back? Did someone come for you?"

"Oh, no. They repaired the rudder for me, and my instruments, and I flew home a few days later."

"In clear weather, I hope."

"Yes. It was beautiful the whole way. Of course I had to make my deliveries first."

"Your father must have been proud of you."

"He was, but in a way it was what he expected of me. It was what he would have done. Figured out a way to get down."

"I hope it never happened again."

"No, there have been other minor emergencies. But nothing like that."

"So that's why you're afraid of storms."

"Yes, I keep expecting to be blinded by the lightning and lose my way."

"Not this time."

"No." This time she'd found her way. For a few moments she'd been totally and completely unaware of the storm around her. She raised her head and looked out the window. She saw no lightning or heard any more thunder. The rain had come and was dancing off the windowpanes at an almost horizontal slant. She gave a sigh of relief and slid back down next to him.

"I made it through another storm," she said.

"*We* made it," he said.

She closed her eyes and he kissed her eyelids. He put his arms around her and she felt his heart beating in time to hers. Slow and steady after the ride of her life. She wanted to say, *Now what?* But that would spoil everything. So she shut her eyes, and her brain mercifully shut off at the same time. She fell asleep in his arms. She hadn't asked the question, but she knew the answer. *Now what? Now nothing.*

It was still raining the next day. This time she woke ahead of him. She noted the look on his face with satisfaction. He wore a slight smile that lifted the corners of his mouth. She didn't want to wake him, but she couldn't resist placing a quick kiss on his bare shoulder. Then she slid out of his arms and out of the bed.

She winced as her bare feet hit the cold wide planks of the floor. She stood in the middle of the floor, her arms wrapped around her, shivering in the cold air and stared at him, memorizing the angle of his head, the strong line of his jaw and the way his hair fell across his forehead. She told herself she was an idiot to try to memorize him. Not when she was bound to spend the next weeks, months, maybe years, trying to forget him.

She told herself to move on, to get dressed, make breakfast, anything but stare at the man in her bed. The one who would leave her there and return to his real life very soon. Maybe even today. Would he ever think of her? Would he try to forget? What did it matter?

She got dressed quietly and went to the kitchen. She was bursting with energy. She felt as if she'd drunk a double espresso, when she hadn't even plugged in the coffeemaker yet. She stirred up a pan of biscuits, put them in the oven, then started some bacon frying and beat some eggs to scramble.

When the doorbell rang, she hurried to the door. It was Melvin Stuart standing in the rain. She motioned him to come in.

"Hi, there, Carrie. Looks like the lightning just missed you." He nodded at the fallen tree. "Doctor still here?"

"Yes. There's no way he could get out, Mel. Why? You're not sick, are you?"

"No, I just came to tell you you've got your power restored. Say, but what if I was sick? Who'd take care of me?"

"I know. I know. We need a nurse."

"Why have a nurse when we could get a doctor?"

"But there's no way we can get a doctor to come

up here to live. First, in a town our size, he couldn't make a living. Second, most doctors, like most people, don't want to live at the edge of the world. I do and you do and most of the rest of us love it here. But you can imagine how it looks to an outsider.''

Carrie didn't need to use any imagination to know that. Her former fiancé had put it plainly: *I knew it would be isolated. I knew it would be primitive. But I didn't know it would be so…so….*

He hadn't needed to finish his sentence. She could have finished it for him. She did finish it for him in her mind. *So isolated, so lonely, so…so boring.*

''How can a person sleep with those good smells coming up the stairs?'' he asked. She spun around and gaped at Matt in his bare feet, old jeans and the T-shirt he'd worn when he came, that she'd washed for him. He was framed in the doorway of the living room, leaning against the woodwork, looking sexier than any man had a right to look first thing in the morning.

She thought she'd be prepared to see him. She thought she'd be over that throbbing, heart-palpitating excitement this morning. But it was back like a quick ride on a roller coaster.

''Hi,'' she said breathlessly. ''Uh, this is Melvin— he's the one who got our power back on. Melvin, I don't believe you've met Dr. Baker.''

Matt shook Melvin's hand and told him to call him Matt. Melvin stepped into the living room leaving wet footprints on the carpet.

''Thanks for coming, Mel,'' she said, hoping he'd turn around and leave without conveying his message to Matt. There was no point in asking the impossible.

She knew the answer, and now Mel knew the answer. She went back to the door, even putting her hand on the handle. Surely he'd get the hint.

"Could I ask you a question, Doc?" he said.

"Sure."

Reluctantly Carrie stepped away from the door. She couldn't help but think of the breakfast getting cold in the kitchen while Mel prepared to ask Matt for the impossible—that he set up a practice in Mystic.

"See," he said to Matt as he took off his broad-brimmed rain hat and held it in his hands while it dripped on the floor. "We need a doctor in town, and we were wondering, that is some of us were talking at the store this morning, wondering if we could hire you as our doctor."

Carrie felt her face turn red with embarrassment. Poor Mel, thinking he could coax a future plastic surgeon to give up a brilliant career to practice medicine in Mystic. She knew Matt would be polite. She knew he'd be tactful, but still...

"I'm very flattered," Matt said. "I know what a great community you have up here and you wouldn't invite just anybody to be a part of it. But I have a job in San Francisco. I'm going to begin a residency in plastic surgery. It's something I've been preparing for for years. They're expecting me and I really have to get back there as soon as I can."

"Oh, I was afraid of that," Mel said. "Well, if you know anybody who needs a job, let us know. Or let Carrie know. You'll be in touch, won't you?" He looked from Carrie to Matt and back again.

"Of course," Matt said. "There are doctors who

specialize in family medicine, which is what you need. Or a nurse practitioner.''

Melvin nodded and reluctantly said goodbye.

Carrie held the door open for him. ''I told him before you came down. He already knew what you'd say. I don't know what he was thinking, you working here. But he just had to hear it from you.''

''I'm really sorry to disappoint him. Maybe I can find you someone,'' Matt said.

''Someone who'd come up to live in Mystic and practice medicine?'' she asked incredulously.

''Maybe it wouldn't be a doctor, but some kind of medic who'd appreciate the town as much as you do. Who loves the outdoors and the independent way of life. Come on, Carrie, you don't think you're the only one who values this place.''

''Of course not, but...'' She didn't finish her sentence. This was not the time to debate this subject again. Instead she led the way to the kitchen. She thought she'd be embarrassed to see Matt this morning. She thought she'd be tongue-tied and shy. But when they got to the kitchen where the stove heated the room and the smell of hot biscuits filled the air, and he took her in his arms in the kitchen and held her close and kissed her forehead, her cheeks and then her lips, she forgot all that, let herself go and gave a sigh of pure contentment.

''I missed you this morning,'' he murmured into her ear. ''I wanted to wake you up with a kiss and make love to you again to show you it wasn't just the lightning and thunder. I wanted to kiss all the places I missed last night.''

"Really?" she murmured. "I didn't think you missed any."

"Hmm. You know, if I wasn't so hungry right now, I'd take you back up there and…"

She wrapped her arms around his neck and pressed her lips against his mouth. Yes, she wanted to hear him say what he wanted to do, but even more she wanted to wrap her body around his, to breathe in the essence of him, to absorb him into her pores. If she'd stayed in bed, woke him up with a kiss, would they be there now, the sheets tangled around them, their bodies pressed against each other, cheek to cheek, hip to hip.

She shivered. If she thought that one night with him would be enough, she knew now she was wrong. One night had made her wish for another, and another would only make her wish for more. So she had to stop now before she was in over her head. After he left, she'd be left to pick up the pieces. Now was the time to think of the future and try not to make it any harder than it was going to be on herself.

"Breakfast," she said brightly, pulling out of his arms. "I'm hungry, too."

He nodded, but he gave her a quick glance as if he knew why she'd changed the subject. As if he'd read her thoughts and not only shared them but reached the same conclusion. Back off. Yes, last night had been special. Yes, they both wanted more, but that would only make it harder to say goodbye. Speaking of goodbye…

"I was listening to the weather report on the radio before you came down," she said as she poured two cups of coffee and sat down at the table across from him.

He was so busy spreading butter on a hot, flaky biscuit he didn't even look up.

"They say it will clear tomorrow," she said.

"Already?" he said.

"Already? You've already been here two days and seven hours longer than you or anyone else planned. Aren't you going stir crazy?" she asked.

He shook his head. "If I only have one more day," he said soberly. "I want to make the most of it."

She nodded. She didn't think he'd jump for joy, but she did think he'd be moderately happy at the thought of leaving. After all, he had a life to get back to. But there was no hint of joy or relief in his voice.

"Of course. What do you want to do?" As soon as she'd spoken the words, she was sorry. He gave her a long, steady look that told her she knew exactly what he wanted to do.

"Matt," she said, setting her fork down. "Last night was—"

He held up his hand. "I know what you're going to say," he said. "It was nice but... Don't worry, I understand. You don't want to spend the day in bed with me."

"Wait, I never said..."

"You didn't have to. Your face is so expressive, Carrie, you have no idea." He reached across the table and rubbed his knuckles gently across her cheek. "I can tell what you're thinking. I guess I knew deep down, when you were gone this morning, that was it. You were sending me a message. I got it and you're right. We both have lives to live after tomorrow. I'm not saying I agree with you, but I respect your opinion. But I wish…''

She held perfectly still, her gaze locked on his, waiting for him to say what he wished. But he didn't. He shook his head and set his fork down.

''Any more coffee?'' he asked.

She got up and filled his cup. She set the coffeepot down and stood behind him with her hands on his shoulders. She was preparing some kind of speech. She wanted to say something that would let him know how much this interlude had meant to her, how she felt about him and how much she'd miss him. But before she could speak, the doorbell rang again. She dropped her hands. He turned his head and looked up at her inquiringly.

She sighed. Was it from relief that she didn't have to make her speech? Or concern that she might not be able to say what was in her heart? She only knew she was off the hook for now. ''I have no idea who that could be. You stay here and finish your breakfast,'' she said.

Matt sat at the kitchen table and looked up at the clock on the wall. How much time did they have left together? Whatever it was, it wasn't enough. Or maybe it was too much. He had no idea how hard it was going to be to get back to his other life. He only knew he would miss her terribly. Sometime during the day, he had to tell her how much she'd meant to him. How tempted he was to say yes to Melvin's request.

He looked around the kitchen at the hand-painted designs on the cupboards and the copper pots on the stove. He knew how much love and care had gone into the furnishing and the building of this room and this house. Every inch reflected Carrie's personality. He inhaled the fragrance of coffee and hot biscuits and homemade jam.

He could imagine without any trouble what it would be like to live here with her. Making love every night in front of the fireplace. Long, leisurely mornings in bed. Life took on a different rhythm up here. There was time for family and friends. Lots of time. There was even time for fishing and boating in this vast and wild land.

He could very well be the town doctor as Melvin and others had suggested. He could handle emergencies here and in other nearby villages that Carrie would fly him to. But what would happen if he woke up one day and realized he hadn't fulfilled his destiny? How would he feel knowing there were no other doctors to talk to, to learn from, to share ideas with? That there was no hospital, no equipment. There was just himself.

He would be Carrie's husband, the man who gave up his career for her. She was worth it, no doubt about it. She was everything he'd ever wanted but didn't know it. He hadn't known anyone like her even existed. Now that he knew, how was he ever going to be happy with anyone else? He wasn't. But if he gave up his career for her, whether she'd asked him to or not, the day would come when he'd resent her for it, and that wouldn't be fair.

He knew, as surely as he knew he was meant to be a doctor, that there would be no other woman for him. As soon as he got back to California, he had an obligation to inform Mira he wasn't going to marry her.

He couldn't. Not now, not ever. He didn't intend to tell the truth, that he'd met a woman who'd spoiled him for all others. No, he'd make up something more believable. He'd use his work as an excuse again. That excuse had worked in the past, it would work again.

When Carrie came back to the kitchen, he was more than ever determined to make the most of this day and not spoil it by thinking of the future or what might have been.

"You have another patient," she said with a smile.

"Nothing serious, I hope," he said, getting up from the table.

"How are you at broken bones?" she asked.

He shrugged. "It's been a while, but I'll do what I can. Who is it? How did it happen?"

"The patient's name is Ruby and she had a run-in with a door."

"That's how she broke her leg?" he asked.

"That's what they say."

Matt followed Carrie into the living room where a young girl was sitting in the overstuffed chair with a cardboard box at her feet. She didn't seem to be in pain, nor could he see any broken bones, offhand.

"Angela, this is Dr. Baker."

Angela nodded shyly.

"What's the problem, Angela," he asked, kneeling down next to her.

"It's Ruby," she said, her eyes filling with tears. "She broke her leg." She lifted the top off the box to reveal a lop-eared rabbit inside resting on a bed of wood shavings.

Matt smiled reassuringly at the little girl, and with

two hands, he lifted the rabbit gently out of the box and ran his fingers over the back leg, trying to determine which bones were involved. The rabbit was shaking in his hands, probably from fear or shock.

"I'm not sure if this is a strain or an incomplete fracture. Without an X ray, it's hard to tell. To be on the safe side, we'll treat it as a fracture. It was good that you brought your rabbit to see me," he said to Angela.

"But you can fix him, can't you?" Angela asked hopefully, looking at him with huge brown eyes.

"I can try," Matt said. "I'm not an orthopedic man, that's a doctor who treats broken bones, but I'll see what I can do. Carrie, could you get my case for me?

"What we want to do with a broken bone is to put it back in place until it heals itself. Bones will do that if we help them along," he explained. He looked inside the ship's doctor's case and found his package of tongue depressors. After gently pushing the bone back into place he took a roll of gauze and wrapped a wooden tongue depressor around the leg. Then he sealed it with adhesive tape and handed Ruby to her owner.

"Ruby should stay off her feet for a while while the bone heals," he said. "Can you keep her from hopping around?"

Angela nodded vigorously, hugging the bunny to her chest.

"Wait, I'm going to give her a shot of vitamin B-complex just to boost her general health and so she'll feel better. You hold her tight, Angela." He took out a disposable syringe, filled it with the liquid vitamin and inserted the needle into the rabbit's haunch. After a brief shudder, the rabbit relaxed into Angela's arms.

"What if she doesn't get better?" Angela asked, and bit her lower lip.

"I think she will, but just in case, I'll give you my phone number, and you can call me and maybe I can suggest something for you to do," Matt said.

"Thank you," the little girl said as she put the rabbit back into the box.

"How will you get her home?" Matt asked.

"Her mom is waiting in the car outside," Carrie said.

Matt stood in the doorway with Carrie, watching Angela carry her precious rabbit in its box out to the waiting car. Then he went to the bathroom to wash his hands. When he came back, Carrie was standing at the window watching the sky, reminding him of when he had to leave this place.

"You're amazing," Carrie said, turning to give him a smile.

"Just call me Dr. Dolittle," he said.

"This is your vacation. You weren't supposed to be working."

"That wasn't work. That was fun. Cute kid."

"I don't suppose you had a rabbit when you were a kid, considering you had a disadvantaged childhood," she teased.

"That's right," he said. "No fishing, no siblings, no pets."

"What did you do for fun?"

"Fun? That's a good question. Let's see. I entered the science fair and won second prize for my project on inchworms."

"That was fun?"

"For me it was. I was a serious kid. What about you?"

Carrie leaned back against the wall while the images came to her mind—planting a garden in the spring, following a red fox to learn where its den was, building a fort in the fir tree behind the house. What a free and happy childhood it had been. "Oh, I had lots of fun, running wild in the woods with the other kids. My friends and I also had a very exclusive club and we met in our tree house out in back." She glanced out the window. "I'm just glad the storm didn't get that one. Yes, in some ways we did things just like kids all over the country. Except you, of course."

"Me? I guess I was really different. What can I say? I was a real nerd. A dork. By the way, what happened to the other kids, the friends you grew up with? I haven't seen many people your age around," he said, sitting on the arm of the big chair.

"They're mostly all gone, like young people in small towns everywhere, they had to leave to find jobs on the outside. I was the only one to go on to school, though. After high school some of my friends went to work at the zinc mine up north, some went to Juneau to work in government offices and a few stayed around to fish and hunt. You're right, there are only a few my age." She was afraid he was going to ask her again about loneliness and she was ready to deny it once again. "Which doesn't bother me," she said before he could phrase the question. "Because I have plenty of friends of all ages—kids and old people, too. Well, you know, you've been meeting them."

"Stan, for example," he said.

"Yes, Stan. Though he's not originally from here."
But he fitted in there. She knew that. He was a good
and decent man and he was an excellent craftsman.
He'd make some woman a wonderful, thoughtful and
kind husband. But not her. She was more convinced
than ever she'd never marry. How could she when no
one could match Matt? It wouldn't be fair to the man
to be second best. Stan should marry someone who
adored him. He would, too, eventually, though he
might have to do some searching.

After Matt left she'd make sure Stan was under no
false illusions. She'd have to make it clear to him she
had no interest in being more than a friend to him.
She should have done it long ago, but now that she
knew for sure what she wanted—she knew it wasn't
him. She could get depressed if she thought about
what she wanted and what she couldn't have, but this
was Matt's last day, so she was going to be upbeat
and cheerful, no matter how hard it was.

"We should make the most of this day," she said,
then she blushed, remembering what he'd proposed
doing today. "I mean, there's only one thing on my
calendar, and that's the faculty-student high school
basketball game."

"That should be fun," he said.

"How would you feel about playing?" she asked.

"What? I don't think I fit into either category, faculty or student."

"I don't, either, but I'm playing. You see, the en-
tire faculty is only six teachers, so they supplement
with any other adult they can con into playing. I know

they're short, so I thought maybe you wouldn't mind. Even if you've never played before.''

''Who said I've never played basketball?'' he said. ''I was never a star, but I was on the junior varsity in high school.''

''You, the nerd, the dork, you played on the team?'' she asked. ''I would have thought you'd have been too busy working on your science fair project.''

''I confess my parents didn't want me playing. They thought I should be working on something, anything but going to practices after school, but the coach asked me to join and I was so excited to be wanted, I said I would. He probably only asked me because I was tall, not because I had any talent. Anyway, I usually sat on the bench, but I liked the other guys, I enjoyed the camaraderie, and once I even made a three-pointer.''

''Really? Wait till the team hears this. I'm bringing a ringer. Maybe the faculty will win for once.''

''I don't know what I'd wear.''

''I'll check my dad's closet. I'm sure he's got a pair of shorts and some old rubber-soled shoes. Oh, one more thing. I promised to bake cookies for the bake sale before the game. Other than that, I'm all yours.'' Again she blushed. Everything she said, every thought that ran through her mind had something to do with making love to Matt.

A smile caught at the corner of his mouth. In a flash he crossed the room and trapped her against the wall with his hands braced next to her shoulders.

''Say that again,'' he said in a deep husky voice that made her knees weak.

She didn't want to say it again. She wanted to take

back the words, but with his laser gaze on hers, pinning her to the wall as effectively as his arms were, she couldn't.

''I'm all yours,'' she breathed softly.

He was so close, so tantalizingly close to her she could feel the heat from his body, smell the coffee on his breath and the antiseptic on his hands. Maybe she was wrong to turn down his offer. Maybe they ought to run back up to the bedroom. Maybe this was her last chance to make love with a man she loved. Loved? How could she fall in love with a man in two days? It wasn't possible. And yet if this wasn't love, what was?

No, she was just trying to give herself an excuse for making love to Matt. She couldn't, wouldn't, shouldn't do anything she'd regret later, any more than what she'd done already. But for the life of her, at that moment in time she couldn't see what harm a kiss would do. Especially when he was nibbling so gently at her lips, tempting, coaxing her until she parted her lips and allowed his tongue to resume the dance they'd started only a short time ago.

She was conscious of the wall behind her, pressing into her back. She wasn't conscious of much more than that other than his mouth on hers. Her tongue wrapped around his. She knew he'd never try to change her mind about returning to bed. He respected her too much. But he also desired her. She saw all that for a split second before she closed her eyes. It was her last coherent thought before he captured her mouth with his.

Desire flared in her belly, so strong and so earth-shaking she felt her knees give way. If he hadn't caught her around the waist, she would have sunk to the floor in a heap. But he did. He held her to him, crushing her breasts against his hard chest. Then he deepened the kiss until she felt it all the way to her toes.

She heard someone moan. It could have been her. It could have been him. It could have been both of them.

After an eternity of out-and-out mind-numbing ecstasy, he pulled back. She felt lost and deserted. She grabbed on to his shoulders and buried her face in his shirt.

"I want you, Carrie," he said in a low voice that made her tremble inside and out. "I've wanted you all my life. I just didn't know it."

She let out a shaky sigh. As if it mattered what he wanted. As long as he couldn't have it, couldn't have her without giving up the rest of his life, he was not going to have her and she was not going to have him. She didn't say that. She just murmured something unintelligible and finally, finally, lifted her head and let her arms drop.

She supposed she ought to respond to his statement, but she had no idea what to say. She could tell him she'd wanted him all her life, too. But what was the point? She couldn't have him. It was better to let it go. Which is what she did. She muttered something about getting ready, slipped out from under his arms and went upstairs.

Chapter Nine

She found a pair of her dad's shorts for Matt to wear to the basketball game and a pair of beat-up high-top gym shoes and put them into a duffel bag. Then she collected her own outfit, as well. They drove to town without saying much. He appeared to be lost in his thoughts. She stared at the road ahead while his words echoed through her brain.

I've wanted you all my life, I just didn't know it. What could she say to that? That she felt the same way? What good would that do? It would just make it that much harder to say goodbye. She felt the tension between them but didn't know how to break it. Was it because she'd left his declaration hanging there in the air? Was he sorry he'd said anything? What more was there to say? She dropped him off at Donny's house. He said he'd meet her at the library and she nodded in agreement. She told him the game was at three o'clock.

It was a relief to get back to her routine. The calm, quiet atmosphere of the library was soothing to her frayed nerves. Once she'd opened the door to the library, put the returned books back on the shelves and cataloged some new donations, she felt more like herself. Yes, it would be hard to adjust when Matt was gone, but she knew she could do it. Life would go on just as it always had. Plus, she'd have her work. She'd be back out flying. When Maggie came in, she was feeling almost cheerful, not the least bit jealous of her clothes or her hair or her way with men and asked her how she liked the mystery she'd checked out the last time.

Maggie said she liked it fine, then tilted her head and gave Carrie a swift look and asked Carrie a question of her own. "How did you like the ring? Oh, I see you're wearing it. Yes, it suits you, I knew it would."

Carrie held out her hand and looked at her ring. "It's beautiful. Thanks for suggesting it."

"I didn't," Maggie said. "I showed him everything I had and he picked it out. That man has good taste. But you know that. He also has some very strong ideas about what he likes, and he likes you."

Carrie gave her a faint smile. "I like him, too," she said quietly.

"Do you?" Maggie asked. "What are you going to do about it?"

"Nothing," Carrie said. "There's nothing I can do."

"Oh, come on," Maggie said. "What do you mean nothing? If I had a man around who bought me jewelry and came all the way up here to see me..."

"He didn't come to see me," Carrie protested. "He came to see Donny. That's the only reason he's here."

"Maybe he came to see Donny, but he's staying to see you," Maggie said.

"No, no. He's staying because he can't get out," Carrie said with a glance out the window. "I can't fly in this kind of weather, but maybe tomorrow…at least that's what I'm hoping."

"Sure you are," Maggie said. "The most attractive man that's ever hit Mystic is stuck here with you at your house and you're hoping he'll leave tomorrow. Pardon me if I'm a little skeptical."

"I'm serious. He has to get on with his life and so do I. This weather delay has me backed up with my deliveries. And Matt is supposed to report for his residency."

"I know, he told me," Maggie said. "I love a man who's dedicated to something, don't you? Something selfless, something altruistic, some way of serving mankind. Something beyond money and recognition. I tell you if he looked at me the way he looks at you. If he bought me a ring like the one he bought you, I'd think of something. I wouldn't let him go."

"What do you suggest, Maggie?" Carrie asked a little stiffly.

"I don't know. What about puncturing a tire on your floatplane or putting a little sugar in the gas tank. He'd never know, and you'd have another few days together."

Carrie's mouth fell open in astonishment. "I can't believe you'd suggest such a thing. I could never—"

"Just kidding," Maggie said with a little laugh. "I know you could never, but you asked me what I suggested so I told you. Of course, maybe you want him to leave. Maybe you're tired of him. Maybe you prefer the solitary life of a single woman in the bush. But I don't.''

Carrie didn't know how to respond to that. The first answers that came to her mind were no, no and no. She'd had a taste of companionship and friendship and intimacy, and it only made her want more. All the more reason to end this affair as soon as possible.

Maggie browsed in the shelves for a while, then she left, saying she'd see Carrie at the basketball game, causing Carrie to wonder why she'd come in in the first place. She had the feeling her real purpose was to talk about Matt. How long would it be before it was all over town that Matt was leaving tomorrow and that Carrie wasn't really interested in Matt after all. Carrie supposed that was better than having the whole town think she'd fallen in love with him and would be suffering from a broken heart when he left. Of all things Carrie wanted to avoid, pity was first on the list.

When Matt came to the library, it was empty except for Carrie. The few patrons who'd wandered in to peruse the books and get caught up on the latest gossip had gone home to lunch. Matt told her he'd said goodbye to the family, left some medicine, his phone number and instructions, presuming that he'd be leaving tomorrow.

She nodded. ''I called the weather people in Anchorage and they're predicting clear skies down here. I think it's pretty safe to assume we can get out and I can take you to Juneau. Hopefully you can get a flight to San Francisco.''

He nodded soberly. ''I'll call the airline,'' he said, but instead of picking up the phone on her desk he sat on the edge of a small, scarred table that had been given to the library by one of the residents when he moved out of town.

"How was Donny today?" she asked.

"I see some improvement in his reflexes. That's a good sign. The swelling must be going down. If he continues to improve, he can be moved out to a hospital in a few weeks. That would be the best thing."

"I wish I could bring him down myself, but it would take so many stops for refueling, and it would be a long and tedious trip for somebody who's flat on his back. A floatplane is ideal for what I do up here, landing on water everywhere I go, but it's totally impractical to go any long distance. The floats slow the plane down because of the wind drag. If it were only me...but I can't take Donny in my plane. Instead I'll find him a real med-evac plane. Where's the best place to take him?" Carrie asked.

"The best place is San Francisco where I know the neurosurgeon."

"That might be expensive," Carrie said with a frown. She knew the family had no health insurance and could never afford the kind of care Matt was talking about.

"Don't worry about the money. If you can get him down there, I'll figure out a way to pay for his care."

"That would be wonderful," she said. She was so touched she felt a tear spring to her eye. She bent her head and thumbed the pages of the book on her desk so he wouldn't notice. But he did notice. He moved to her desk and tilted her chin with his thumb.

"It's going to work out," he said. "Don't worry."

"I know. I have confidence in you. I just…I'm just so touched that you'd go to all this trouble."

"You're the one who's gone to all the trouble. You came and got me. You're going to arrange for his transportation."

"Yes, but he's like one of the family. When somebody's hurt or needs help, we all rally around."

"Yes, I know. I've seen it."

"But you never knew him before. You have no reason to go out of your way to help him. And yet you're doing it."

"Come on, Carrie. Any other doctor would do the same if he could."

She nodded, but she didn't believe it. How many other doctors had she tried before she got to the ship? Not that they weren't concerned, they just couldn't interrupt their schedules.

"About the game," she said. "Are you still up for it?"

He said he was. They went back to her house for lunch, and Carrie made a batch of brownies for the potluck supper that would follow the game. They both carefully steered away from saying anything personal and were back at the school to suit up for the game before three.

Before the game started, Carrie was sitting on the home team bench in the bleachers next to Maggie. When Matt walked across the polished floor in his shorts, Carrie heard Maggie give a soft whistle of appreciation.

"All that and a medical degree, too," Maggie said softly but not too softly for Carrie to hear. Carrie didn't blame her for staring at Matt's muscular legs.

After all, he was without doubt the most attractive man who'd come to Mystic in years, maybe ever. She also had to admit Maggie looked great as usual. She was wearing very short shorts that showed off her long shapely legs, and a tight T-shirt with her hair pulled back in a ponytail. She looked almost as young as the high school girls and twice as pretty.

Carrie herself tried to look everywhere but at Matt. But if she'd avoided looking at him, she would have been the only one in the whole place. Her eyes followed him up and down the polished boards along with everyone else. After all, he was a novelty. The buzz in the gym among the students was that he was the faculty's secret weapon, which made him a natural object of everyone's interest. Not only that, but she was sure the rumor mill had them practically engaged. She and Maggie went out on the floor to warm up and the students let loose with good-natured boos and hisses.

Carrie knew it was because he was new in town that everyone watched him. It was also that he'd already established himself as a generous and all-round nice guy. But that wasn't why Carrie's eyes followed him wherever he went. Or why she dropped the ball when it was passed to her. She could no more look elsewhere than she could fly to the moon. In a few short days she'd fallen for him so hard she knew deep down that she was not going to get over him as fast as she'd told herself she would.

But she would get over him. She had to. She could not spend the rest of her life thinking about him, wondering how he was, who he was with. If he'd married or become as successful as his father. One of the teachers slapped her on the back for encouragement and she was jarred back into the present. She finally stopped staring at Matt and focused on catching the ball instead.

When the game started, she knew the adults would lose. They always did. Their experience was no match for the youthful skill and energy. But no one cared who won except for the students. It was all about school spirit. Town spirit. Alaska spirit. The kids in the bleachers waved pom-poms, they screamed and they sang their school song. They cheered when the school principal stumbled and fell on the floor. He picked himself up and acknowledged their cheers with a good-natured wave and the kids went crazy again. They yelled themselves hoarse when the sixth-grade teacher bumped into the wall.

When the principal, who served also as the coach, beckoned Carrie to go into the game in place of the kindergarten teacher, she dribbled the ball slowly down the floor. She'd always loved basketball. It was the perfect sport for kids who lived in Alaska. Even the poorest village had a school and a gym. The gyms were open year-round after school and evenings for the kids to practice their shots and pickup games. It was a way of getting exercise during the worst winter weather. The regional championships were the highlight of the winter season. As for the state tournaments, it was every Alaska kid's dream, both girls' and boys', to go to the Big Four in Anchorage. In college, Carrie played intermural basketball. But it was nothing like basketball in her hometown or her home state.

Carrie passed the ball to Matt. He passed it back.

She ran down the court to the basket and threw the ball. To her amazement, it went in. The kids booed again. Matt grinned at her and slapped her on the back. She grinned. The other teachers yelled at her, "Nice shot."

The faculty was ahead. She knew it wouldn't last. The students were younger, taller, faster and practiced more, but she was ridiculously proud of her shot. Did it have anything to do with Matt being there, sharing the moment, contributing to her success? She had to admit it did.

The next time it was Matt's turn for a free throw. She shut her eyes as she stood on the court. It meant nothing. It was a silly, just-for-fun game, not important in the grand scheme of things, and yet it was. She wanted him to make the shot. She wanted him to succeed. She wanted the former nerd and dork to show the town of Mystic he was more than a doctor. Most of all, she wanted him to show himself he could do it. She heard, rather than saw, the ball swish through the basket. She opened her eyes and clapped so loud her hands hurt.

It was the best faculty-student game ever. That's what everyone said. Yes, the students won, as usual. Allison herself made fifteen points on the coed student team. But it was close. For the first time, the adults gave the kids a run for their money. When the game was over and the committee was setting up for the potluck supper, Zach Stuart, the principal, told Matt how glad he was he'd come to help them out.

"The kids are complaining we've brought in a ringer," he said with a grin. "But as long as they won, they're happy."

Matt was exhausted. His face was dripping, his shirt and shorts stuck to his body. He'd run steadily for most of the game. He'd made a few shots after that free throw and despite his fatigue, he felt euphoric. He knew if he had a child, he'd want her or him to enjoy a wide range of activities. Not just science fairs, but sports, too.

After he'd showered and changed, he looked around the gym for Carrie. Seeing her run up and down the floor in her shorts had been one of the pluses of the game. She looked so cute and so full of energy and enthusiasm, he couldn't believe she was thirty years old. When she made a shot or a good pass, he wanted to hug her. But he didn't.

He found her behind the buffet table stirring a pot of stew.

"You were great," he said, wanting to hug her right now. Wanting to drag her away behind the gym and make out with her the way the high school kids did. The way other high school kids did. But not him. No wonder his hormones were raging now when he was in his thirties. He'd skipped that whole phase in high school. He had years to make up for. "You didn't tell me you'd played on the school team. I had to hear it from someone else."

"You didn't ask me. And I didn't know if I could still play. Once a year isn't enough to keep in shape."

He let his gaze slide over the sweater and slacks she'd changed into. "I'd say you've managed pretty well."

"So have you," she said. But she didn't look at him, she looked down at the carrots and chunks of beef in the bubbling pot.

"It was fun," he said.

Before she could say anything else, Maggie came up and shook Matt's hand and told him what a great game he'd played. When she asked him to help her set up the folding tables and chairs, he couldn't refuse. Even though he would rather have stood there and watched Carrie toss salad.

"I hear you'll be leaving us tomorrow," she said.

"If the weather clears," he said calmly. But inside he was far from calm. A sinking feeling hit him just when he thought he'd come to terms with leaving tomorrow. He'd tried to ignore it, tried not to think about leaving, tried to accept his imminent departure with as much equanimity as possible, but every hour that passed, every shared moment with Carrie made it harder and harder. He didn't want to talk about it, but what else could he do when someone else brought it up.

"We'll miss you," Maggie said, handing him a folding chair to set next to the table.

"I'll miss you all," he said.

"Especially Carrie, I suppose," she said.

"Yes, of course," he said.

"She's an amazing person. So self-sufficient. Just like her father. Doesn't need anyone. I don't understand her. I never have. I'm the type who likes company. We have long, cold winter nights up here. It can get pretty lonely," she said.

"I can imagine," he said. But Carrie had said she was never lonely. Not in a friendly town like this one. But he could easily imagine spending those long, cold nights with Carrie. Nights like last night.

"Of course, there are plenty of men who'd like to spend them with her. You've met Stan, I suppose."

"Yes."

"He follows her around like a puppy dog, but she doesn't even notice."

"Right. Well, let me carry this table, Maggie." He walked away from her, table in hand, to set it up by himself. He didn't want to hear her talk about Carrie. He knew she was self-sufficient. He didn't know if it made him feel better or worse about leaving. All in all, despite the general hilarity, the fun of playing basketball and lighthearted atmosphere in the gym, he was starting to feel pretty terrible.

Carrie was one of the servers, so he didn't even get to sit next to her. He watched her from where he sat with the principal and his wife and found it hard to pay attention to the conversation around him. When everyone else had been served, he saw Carrie fill her plate and go to another table. It looked like she was sitting next to Stan. Stan's face was all smiles. Matt didn't blame him. He'd be smiling too if he had her at his side. Stan was obviously crazy about her. Would she someday realize that life with him was better than life alone up here? He looked down at the food on his plate and realized he couldn't eat another bite. It suddenly tasted like sawdust.

He mumbled some excuse about getting some coffee, got up and went outside. He took a deep breath of cool air and felt a little better but not much. A glance at the sky showed clouds moving and patches of pale blue. The first star had come out. The first star he'd seen since he'd arrived there. Yes, the weather was changing. He ought to be glad. But he wasn't.

When Carrie came out and joined him with the duffel bag in her hands, she looked worried.

"I saw you leave. Are you okay?"

"Fine," he assured her. "Just needed some air."

"Let's go home," she said, putting her hand on his arm. "You look tired."

"Whatever you want," he said. Let's go home, she'd said. But it wasn't his home. It was hers. He didn't have a home. There was his parents' home, but he'd lived in rented apartments ever since he started medical school.

Back at her house, he called the airline and got a reservation for a flight from Juneau to San Francisco tomorrow afternoon. It was all happening so fast. He thought he'd have time to prepare himself mentally to leave, but he didn't. Maybe he'd never be ready. Yet at the same time he didn't know what to do with the time remaining. He knew what he wanted to do, but he also knew it was out of the question to spend another night in Carrie's bed. One, she had made it clear she didn't want to. And two, if it was anything like last night, he didn't know if he'd be able to leave in the morning.

He needn't have worried about how to spend the evening. Word had gotten around about his departure tomorrow, and the people with aches and pains, chills and fever, and everything in-between, came to Carrie's house for some last-minute consultation. Carrie had them wait in the living room and he saw them in the kitchen. He gave out vitamins and analgesics, but mostly he gave out advice.

"When you have a cold you need to get plenty of rest. Drink lots of liquids. To keep from catching a cold this winter, wash your hands as often as you can. Eat more fruits and vegetables. When you're congested, inhale the steam from a pot of hot water.''

He refused payment, of course, so they came with little gifts for him. They brought small hand-carved animals in the shape of bear and moose or miniature hand-painted totem poles. It was after ten o'clock when the last grateful patient left.

"Thanks a lot, Doc," Marco said as he waved goodbye from the front door. "I'll remember what you said."

"That was quite a turnout," Carrie said as she closed the door behind him. "Did they wear you out?"

"Not at all. I wish I could do more. I hope you didn't mind turning your house into a clinic."

"Of course not."

"I'm glad they felt comfortable enough to come. This kind of medicine is so different from what I'm going to be doing. It's satisfying. You get to know the patients, that is if you live in their community. You know them when they're well and you know them when they're sick. Plastic surgery, as it's practiced by my father, is a whole other thing. His patients come from all over the world because he's a world-renowned specialist. He operates on them, does spectacular things with their faces or hands that can make a huge difference in their lives. When they've healed, they return to their homes and never see him again."

"And that's what you'll be doing?"

"More or less."

"The satisfactions are different, but just as real, I imagine."

"I don't know," he said honestly, sitting on the edge of the couch.

"You look tired," she said.

"For a quiet little village, you know how to keep a visitor busy."

She nodded. "It's not always like this."

"I've had a good time," he said simply.

"I know." She paused. Her gaze collided with his, then she looked around the room, anywhere but at him. "I'll get you a blanket and pillow."

There it was. The words he knew were coming but didn't really want to hear. Of course he knew it had been decided, a mutual decision, he told himself, that what happened last night between them would not be repeated. It was in both of their interests to let it rest, to forget it ever happened, and most of all, not to repeat it.

He didn't look up, he was afraid to look in her eyes and see nothing but embarrassment. No memories, no longing, no desire. But, he hoped, no regrets either. In any case, she set the bedding on the couch, checked the sky once more, told him it looked clear and said goodnight.

He watched her walk up the stairs. Then the house was quiet. Too quiet. No wind outside. No sounds inside. She must have fallen asleep instantly. More power to her. He undressed and lay down but he was sure he wouldn't sleep at all. His brain was wide awake. The images floated in front of his face though his eyes were closed.

Carrie with the sun shining on her dazzling copper-colored hair at the dock the first day he saw her.

Carrie with her face over a pot of soup, the steam curling her hair around her face.

Carrie in the hot springs, her whole luscious body pink and warm and so desirable he felt the ache of longing deep inside him. A longing he feared would be with him for a long, long time.

Carrie panting while she raced down the basketball court in shorts and a T-shirt.

Carrie in bed with him, her face aglow, her body arched toward him. He turned over and buried his face in his pillow. But the images wouldn't stop. His imagination was working overtime. He now imagined he could hear her moan, hear her call his name. But he couldn't. She was asleep. He should be, too.

He must have slept because when he woke up it was still dark and he was disoriented, and, for a moment, he didn't know where he was. For a moment, his heart leaped. It was dark. They couldn't fly. But soon he realized the skies were clear. The sun rose, and it was a perfect day for flying.

That's what she said when she came down the stairs. Nothing like, I'm sorry you're leaving. Nothing like, I'll miss you. Just "It's a perfect day for flying." She paused for a moment. "That's not to say the weather couldn't change. Just to be sure, we ought to leave as soon as possible."

"I hope this won't be a totally wasted trip for you," he said. "Taking me all the way to Juneau."

"Not at all. I'll load up the back of the plane with some deliveries and head on over to Ketchikan after I drop you off."

She was all business today. He'd never seen this side of her. It was as if she'd switched from Carrie the hometown girl, the sweet, sexy woman he'd shared a bed with to an accomplished pilot and the head of a small business. She was brisk and efficient, brewing coffee, making toast and eating it while making a list of her freight in duplicate. She scarcely looked at him, made no effort at conversation. She did make a few calls and then she said she was ready. So was he.

The flight was completely smooth. The scenery was spectacular. She pointed out areas of interest. She named the rivers and the mountain range, pointed out villages and towns. She spoke to various control towers on her radio. He looked out the side window, struck by the snow-capped mountains and the vast white empty space.

He tried to appreciate the view. He knew he should be delighted to once again have the opportunity of being in a small plane over this remote state with its spectacular scenery, but he felt numb and cold inside. He was prepared to leave this place, but he wasn't prepared for her change of attitude. Even the look on her face was different. Her eyes were on her controls. Her mouth was set in a straight, determined line. She hadn't smiled all day. He thought he had meant something to her, but he felt now as if he'd never known her at all. He hadn't realized how much that could hurt.

He asked himself what he wanted, how he wanted her to behave, and he had to admit he didn't know. He didn't want tears or sighs or last-minute regrets. Maybe it was better this way. Better for him, better for her. When she landed the plane in the water at the dock in Juneau, a dockhand was waiting. Matt grabbed the black bag he'd borrowed from the ship's doctor and opened the door.

She looked at him then, just a side-glance that told him nothing about how she felt. He leaned over to kiss her goodbye. She turned her head away just in time so his kiss landed on her cheek. He mumbled his thanks, said goodbye and jumped onto the dock with a helping hand from the dockhand. Two hours later, he was in a commercial airplane on his way to San Francisco and another life.

Carrie took off immediately. She allowed herself only a quick glance out the window to see Matt stride across the dock toward the town. She knew he would catch a cab to the airport. She knew he'd be on time for his flight and that even now the memory of these past few days spent with her were fading.

With a fierce effort, she held back the tears until she got her plane into the air, then she let go. She sobbed so loudly she almost missed the message from the radio operator in Ketchikan telling her they were expecting her and that the skies were clear.

She stammered a short reply then wiped her eyes. She'd thought it would help to avoid a tearful good-bye with Matt. She'd thought if she pretended she didn't care whether he left or not, she could convince herself and him that she didn't care. But she did. She cared too much. She felt as if her insides were crumbling. When she got out of the plane she would topple over because there would be nothing left to hold her upright. The tears continued to flow. Better now than while he was there. She'd been holding back for hours, bottling up her feelings and her emotions, and now there was no reason to hold back any longer.

She'd cry all the way to Ketchikan and all the way home and then she'd quit. She'd be all cried out. Dried out with no more tears and no more emotion. She'd face the village and her friends with a smile on her face.

Yes, she'd say. I took him back to civilization. Yes, it was nice to have him here. No, I won't be hearing from him again, except about Donny, of course. And of course I won't be seeing him again. Ever. Yes, he was nice. Yes, he was good-looking. Yes, he was a good doctor. Yes, it was too bad he had to leave.

The more she practiced what she was going to say, the worse she felt. When she finally got home after making her deliveries in Ketchikan, tied up her plane at her dock and went into her house, she felt worse than ever. She only hoped she could avoid seeing anyone, because just a glance in the mirror told her she looked like hell with her red eyes and her pale face.

She knew she should eat something. She was weak and felt hollow inside. But after sharing meals for a few days, eating alone seemed like a miserable alternative. She opened her refrigerator and peered into the freezer. Nothing looked appealing.

She walked into the living room. The fireplace was cold and empty. The fire had gone out in her woodstove. She shivered in the chill of an empty house and almost didn't want to start a fire and make it warm again. Why bother? It was just for her. She was alone. More alone than she'd ever been except after her father died. She got over that, she'd get over this.

She sat on the couch and stared into the ashes in the fireplace thinking of Matt sleeping here where she sat. At least she hoped he'd slept. She hadn't slept at all last night. She'd simply lain in her bed, her head buried in her pillow, counting the hours, wishing it was over. She hated goodbyes. She was glad she'd managed to avoid one with Matt. Maybe he was puzzled at her lack of emotion. By now he would have realized it was the best way. It was the only way. By now he probably wasn't even thinking about her. By now he was back in San Francisco with his girlfriend and his family. Maybe it was time for her to find a boyfriend and start a family of her own.

She tried to picture the face of a man she might marry, but the only face that came to her mind was Matt's. The last look on his face was a puzzled one. Puzzled when she didn't say anything, didn't even try to say what was on her mind. But he must have been grateful, deep down, that she hadn't gone all weepy and emotional on him. Men hated that. She knew because she'd made that mistake with her former fiancé. He'd been embarrassed beyond belief when she tried to tell him how she felt. He just wanted to get out of there—fast.

This time she'd learned her lesson well. This time she'd taken the initiative, given Matt a chance to leave gracefully, which he'd done. Now all she had to do was pick up the pieces and get on with her life. The same life that had been so completely satisfying, so rich and rewarding before she met him. Or had it?

Chapter Ten

Matt called his parents from the airport and they came to get him.

"Thank God you made it back. We've been so worried about you up there in the wilderness all alone," his mother said, giving him a hug.

"There was no need to worry," he said. "I was fine. I wasn't alone. In fact, I was never less alone. It was a fascinating experience."

"I imagine it was," his father said. "You'll have to tell us all about it. Mira's anxious to hear, of course."

Matt opened his mouth to say something about his relationship with Mira, but he didn't. This was not the time to upset his parents. There would be plenty of time later when he'd had time to think up a good excuse. He was afraid "I don't love her" wouldn't quite do it. Instead he asked about his father's health and was relieved to hear his latest EKG was normal but that his father had cut way back on his workload.

"How was the boy you went to treat?" his father asked, as he drove down the freeway toward their house in the suburbs.

"Better. But he needs to be treated as soon as he can be moved. I've spoken to Jay Mercer, and he's agreed to treat him if they can med-evac him down here."

"I'm sure the family was grateful to you. And the woman pilot, what about her?"

Matt didn't know what to say. He knew what he couldn't say: She's the most amazing woman I've ever met. He couldn't ask the question he wanted to ask: Is it possible to fall in love in three days?

"You mean Carrie," he said. "She gave me a tour of the area and showed me a great time." A great time? That was the understatement of the year. He deliberately kept his voice neutral so his parents would read no underlying meaning in that phrase.

"You stayed at her house?" his mother asked a little too casually. Did she know? Could she possibly suspect what had happened while he stayed at her house?

He cleared his throat. "Yes. It's a large house for those parts. But a very small village. No hotels or restaurants. Just a cluster of houses, a school, a volunteer library and even smaller museum."

There was a brief silence while they digested his description. He was sure they couldn't possibly picture the place nor appreciate how simple life was up there nor how good it could be.

"What did you do besides take care of the patient?" his father asked.

Matt was at a loss for words. How to answer such a question? He mumbled something about fishing and sight-seeing in her boat. Then he looked out the window as they drove down his parents' street toward their house. He looked at the large homes surrounded by landscaped grounds, noticing the expensive cars parked in the driveways and was struck by the contrast to the place he'd been. This was the kind of place he'd end up in if he followed in his father's footsteps. The kind of place most people would give anything to end up in. The people here were well-to-do professionals who'd earned the right to a comfortable, even luxurious life with teams of gardeners and house cleaners to keep their property in tip-top shape.

He thought of Mystic and how isolated it was from the outside world when the weather closed in and how the people there dealt with adversity. He thought of the school made up of prefab buildings. He thought of Carrie's kitchen with her handmade drawings decorating her cupboard doors. He thought of the school and the enthusiasm that erupted during a game. He thought of Donny's pleasure at being able to have a chess partner.

"Matt?" his father prompted. "You were telling us what you did up there. You look like you're off in another world."

"Oh, sorry, Dad. I guess I was." He took a moment to collect his thoughts. "What did I do? Oh, not much." *Not much, I just flew over the most spectacular scenery on the earth, I soaked in a hot spring with the most desirable woman I've ever known, and made beautiful love. No, not much. Just a lifetime of experiences, that's all. Was that all? Was that to be the highlight of his life? Would everything be downhill after that? He couldn't believe that. Didn't want to believe that.*

When his father parked in front of their two-story

brick and stone house, he got out of the car and looked around. It looked as strange to him as if he'd been away for years and not days. He almost stumbled on the front steps, and his parents exchanged a worried look.

"It's good you have a few days before the residency starts on Monday," his mother said. "You look like you could use a rest. I'm so sorry you had to miss most of the cruise. We came back completely relaxed."

Matt managed a smile for his mother. "That's good," he said. "I'm really fine. I need to find an apartment in the city near the hospital as soon as possible."

"Of course. But there's no hurry. We love having you around. Of course it's important for you to be close at hand when you're on call."

During the next few days of diligent looking with the help of Mira, Matt found an apartment in the city. It was just a studio a few blocks from the hospital. Mira insisted on helping him not only find it but furnish it, too. Matt felt grateful and also guilty for taking advantage of her. After the furniture had been delivered, she was standing in the doorway with a lamp in her hand, trying to decide where to put it, when he took it out of her hand, put it on an end table and asked her to sit down a moment. It was time, it was past time for him to tell her what he had to say.

She gave him a quick, curious glance and perched on the arm of his new couch while he sat on the edge of the futon. She looked half-apprehensive and half-hopeful. He wouldn't blame her if she thought he was going to propose. He wished he didn't have to do this. He hated to hurt her.

"We've known each other a long time," he said. "Your friendship means a lot to me."

She bit her lip. "I thought it was more than a friendship," she said. "That is, I hoped…"

"Yes, I thought so, too, but I think we'd both know by now if it was meant to be more. I'm afraid we're too comfortable around each other, known each other too long. But it must be as obvious to you as it is to me that we're lucky to have each other as friends and that's how it should be." Lord, he hated this. He didn't want to mention the *M* word, though it was clearly on both their minds.

"Do you think it's bad to feel comfortable around the person you…you…care about?" she asked softly.

"No, of course not," he said. He got up and put his hands on her shoulders. "Mira, you deserve someone better than me."

"There is no one better than you, Matt," she said simply.

He gave her a rueful smile. "You say that now, but it's only because I've monopolized you all these years. You've been brainwashed by my parents and your parents. But you'll find someone who will sweep you off your feet, who will adore you and make a great husband for you."

"That sounds like goodbye," she said.

"Not goodbye. Of course not," he said. "We'll always be friends." Didn't he already say that? In any case, it was true. They probably always would be friends, as long as she wanted to. As long as it didn't keep her from finding someone else.

She nodded and thought for a long moment before she spoke. "What happened to you in Alaska?"

"Happened? I treated a very sick boy who I hope will get better."

"I don't mean that. You've been different ever since you came back."

He knew perfectly well what she meant. He didn't know whether to tell her the truth. He was afraid it would hurt too much. And what was the point? So what if he'd fallen in love with a woman, a way of life and a whole town? He was here now. He was back where he belonged. Yes, he'd changed, but it wouldn't help Mira to know why or how.

"Different or difficult?" he asked. "I'm afraid I haven't been easy to get along with lately. That's why I appreciate all you've done in helping me get set up here. Look at his place." He waved his arm at the new furniture. "It looks great, thanks to you. Now that I'm settled, I can concentrate on my work."

"You have a rough schedule. Maybe when you get used to it…"

He heard the hope in her voice, and he knew it would be cruel to let her think he might change his mind when he knew he wouldn't. "My schedule is going to be rough for the next three years," he said. He knew it was true and he'd wondered more than once in the past few weeks since he'd started, whether it was the right place for him. It wasn't the long hours or the time spent studying after he got back from the hospital, it was the future that worried him. But that was not for Mira to know. Or his parents. Especially not his parents.

This time she understood. There was a sadness and

a hurt in her eyes that made him wish he hadn't had to do this. Or wish he'd done it before now. Because he'd really known it wasn't going to work out before this. He just hadn't faced the fact himself until now.

He stood. "Let me take you out to dinner," he said. "I owe you for all the help you've given me."

"You don't owe me anything," she said a little stiffly. "I loved decorating your place. I only hope... you'll be happy here."

He was sure she was going to say she hoped something else, but she didn't. She politely declined his offer of dinner and left shortly afterward. He was grateful there were no tears, no recriminations, no accusations. He knew there wouldn't be. She was too nice, too sweet, had too much self-control.

He wondered how long it would be before word got back to his parents and they called to tell him he must have lost his mind as well as the most desirable girl in the world. He heated a can of soup on the small stove in his efficiency kitchen and ate it at the kitchen table Mira had chosen. The soup filled his stomach, but in his heart he felt empty and cold. He'd hurt Mira, he'd left Carrie and he was on a professional course he wasn't sure he ought to be on. He told himself this was a period of adjustment. He told himself he'd get used to the work. He'd take it one day at a time and see where it led. As if he didn't know. The examples were all around him. The professors, the surgeons, his father. That was where it all led. To a satisfying, lucrative career.

He'd reached for the phone to call Carrie a dozen times in the week he'd been back. Then he'd put it down. He had legitimate questions to ask about

Donny, but he didn't trust himself to stick to those questions. He was afraid he'd ask Carrie if she missed him as much as he missed her. If she ever thought about him. If she'd ever consider his plan for her to visit San Francisco. He wasn't really afraid to ask the questions, he was afraid to hear the answers.

But he finally made the call on Monday after a grueling day of hospital rounds with the chief plastic surgeon, hours in the O.R. observing surgery, two classes and more hours of studying for an exam the next day.

She didn't answer. He left a message on her answering machine asking her to call him back. Telling her he wanted an update on Donny. He lay on his couch in the living room too tired to sleep, wondering where she was. Imagining her flying over the great empty spaces of the fiftieth state by herself. Was she lonely? Was she afraid of the weather?

No, of course not. She was the bravest person he knew. As for lonely, he remembered how she'd bristled at the very thought. How she'd told him it was impossible to be lonely in the friendliest town in Alaska. Maybe that was true. But Matt knew it was possible to be lonely in the middle of a big city with friends and family and colleagues all around.

There was an ache in his heart, a longing for a deep, intimate connection that could only be satisfied by one special person and if that person wasn't available, for whatever reason, say an accident of geography and family expectations or background, then the ache had to be ignored. There was no pain medicine that would even touch it.

It would go away by itself. It had to go away. He

refused to think he'd have to live his life like this, knowing there was someone out there who could make his life complete but unable to have her.

He had to forget about her. Put the memory of her in a vault, to be taken out and treasured, but only when he felt stronger than he did right now. Right now he had to forget about her. Right after he got the boy down here, got him seen by the right specialists, returned him to the village after he'd been treated with the best care Matt could get for him, and then Matt could really put this whole episode behind him.

That was why he'd called her. That was the only reason. To find out about Donny. That was why he checked his answering machine twenty times the next day. That was why he couldn't concentrate on the study of the maxio-facial structure the way he should. That was why he was vague when he ran into his mother at the hospital on her way to a meeting of the women's auxiliary. She put her hand on his arm and looked at him with a frown.

"Matt, you look terrible," she exclaimed.

He gave her a faint smile. "That's because I haven't slept for twenty-four hours and I had a graham cracker at noon for lunch. I'm an intern, mother, that's how it is. I've been on call for the past three days. I'm not complaining, I'm just telling you we don't get much sleep." He didn't say that even when he got home and tried to sleep, he couldn't. It was partly the noises of the city he was unused to—the ambulance sirens and the garbage trucks, but it was also the fact that his brain wouldn't shut down. His thoughts kept going round and round in his head, always seeking a solution to his problems, but never finding one.

"Don't worry. It won't last forever," his mother said.

No, not forever, just for the next three years. "I know," he said. "Everyone's going through the same thing." Everyone but the doctors who chose not to do a specialty. Who got their M.D. when he did and left to practice general medicine in the boondocks somewhere. As Matt's father said, they traded instant gratification for the challenge of a specialty. Matt was on his way to a lecture so he didn't have time to talk further. It was just as well. Everything he said would just upset her. His mother left, still frowning. Fortunately, there was no time to talk about Mira. He had no idea if his mother had heard he'd broken up with her.

The next weekend he had two days off that he was looking forward to more than he thought possible. He didn't know which was more tired, his brain or his body. He decided to drive up to Yuma, the small town in the foothills of the High Sierras where he'd once done a rotation while still in medical school. He craved the sight of open space and the smell of fresh air. He planned to stop by the clinic where he'd worked, and he thought he might even run into a former patient or two. But mostly he just wanted to walk in the hills, savor the solitude and breathe in the silence.

He checked into a motel, and, after filling his lungs with fresh air that afternoon, he walked to the fifties-style diner on Main Street where he saw one of the doctors he'd worked with. Dr. Brown was delighted to see him and invited Matt to join him and his wife at their table. After Matt brought him up-to-date on his activities, the doctor told him they'd raised enough money to build a new hospital, but needed another doctor to handle the additional load of patients.

"I'd love to practice up here," Matt blurted, surprising himself because up to now he'd known exactly where and what he was going to practice. Plastic surgery in San Francisco.

"I'm afraid we can't afford a plastic surgeon," Dr. Brown said regretfully. "We need someone who can do the basics, set broken bones, treat the run-of-the-mill stuff. Not as exciting or as lucrative as plastic surgery."

Matt nodded. It was true, even though excitement and money were not on the top of his priority list. But he didn't say anything. How could he give up everything he'd been working for? Coming to work as a doctor in this small town would mean giving up everything he'd been destined for since he could remember. He told himself this idea was nothing but a whim, a dream, an excuse to get out of a difficult internship. He could hear his father now, telling him it was the lazy man's way out.

He told Dr. Brown how much he'd enjoyed the small-town atmosphere there in Yuma and recounted his adventures in Alaska. Both the doctor and his wife were fascinated to hear about what he'd done and seen up there. Then Matt asked about various patients he'd treated while working with Dr. Brown and his staff. Since most of the patients were local residents, it wasn't hard for the medical staff to keep track of them.

The next day, Matt accepted Dr. Brown's invitation to stop by to see the new hospital. It was set on a hill on the outskirts of town with a view of the surrounding countryside. Matt and the doctor stood outside on the front of the still-uncompleted building, facing the hills. Matt told the doctor his pride in the new facility was well justified.

"Sure we can't tempt you to join us?" Dr. Brown said with a smile. "You're just the kind of medic we'd like to have around. You not only have the skills we're looking for, we liked the way you related to the patients. They remember you, still ask about you."

Matt was unreasonably pleased to hear that. Of course his father's patients still remembered him, too. Not so much for his personality or his bedside manner, but for the surgery he'd performed. Every time they looked in the mirror, for years afterward, they most likely sent silent thanks to the doctor who'd given them a new look, a new chance at a new life. That was the kind of thing Matt could look forward to.

He told the doctor he was flattered but he was committed to plastic surgery. What was the point of even considering such a radical change of direction? He was trying to imagine life in this town, when he ran into a former patient as he was walking down Main Street that afternoon, a woman whose breech baby he'd delivered one night when Matt had been on call at the old hospital, a small, older brick building right in the middle of town.

Matt had managed to turn the baby around and deliver the baby without having to resort to a C-section. He was happy to see her and her toddler as he strolled down Main Street. She was thrilled to see him and delighted to show off her curly-haired little girl.

After chatting with her for a few minutes and admiring her child, Matt walked on, noticing how different from the city the pace of life was here. It wasn't quite like Mystic, Alaska, but there were some similarities. The friendliness of the natives, the interest they showed in each other and the proximity to nature. That morning he'd gone walking again in the hills. He passed a seasonal stream that would be rushing with water from the Sierras later in the season, and he wondered if there was good fishing there.

Before he left, he went up to the cemetery above the town. He walked from grave to grave, reading the inscriptions on the marble markers and noting the dates. He imagined his own tombstone and wondered what it would say. He wondered who would mourn him when he was gone. And he wondered how many years he had to do what he wanted to do. Not what he had to do, but what he should do.

He went back to the city with renewed energy, determined to face the future without complaining. But the city seemed more crowded and congested than ever. He was stuck in traffic on the bridge for over two hours on his way home to the city. When he got home, there was a message from Carrie. His heart pounded at the sound of her voice. He cursed himself for having been out of town and missing her call. She sounded very cool and calm and collected. She reported on Donny's condition and said she'd be gone for a few days but would try to call him later.

She said nothing at all about missing him. No, of course she wouldn't. Obviously, she had jumped right back into her routine just as he'd done. Or as he'd tried to do. He called her back immediately but got her machine again. Damn, damn, damn. He wanted to talk to her. He wanted to hear something in her voice that told him she missed him, that she cared about him and that she thought about him. Not as much as he thought about her, just one half of that would do. Even a quarter. But she wasn't there.

When he hung up, his mother called to invite him to dinner.

"We want to have an evening of slides of Alaska, yours, ours and Mira's and her parents."

Did she know he'd broken up with Mira? Was this a good time to restore the relationship for what it had always been, one of friendship and nothing more?

"All right," he said. He'd dropped off his slides to be developed but hadn't picked them up. Why? He was busy, that was why. It was not that he was afraid to look at them, afraid the feelings he'd kept bottled up would explode. Afraid that looking at them would bring back too many memories, would call into question everything he was doing, everything he'd planned. No, it was just that he was too busy. Now that they wanted to see them, he'd have no excuse to postpone it. He'd have to put those few days in perspective, treat them as a memory and nothing more.

On Friday evening he picked up his slides and drove to his parents' house. He didn't look at the pictures beforehand, he hadn't had time. He hadn't had time for anything. Not even to think about what he was doing. He felt like a robot, moving from place to place, memorizing, listening, reading, observing, standing on his feet for hours during surgery.

He greeted Mira with a kiss on the cheek. She smiled and murmured something. Her parents were polite but he sensed some stiffness in their part. Maybe he was just imagining it. While setting up the slide projector in the family room, his father asked him how it was going at the hospital. He said fine, but his mother gave him a worried look from across the room where she'd arranged a platter of appetizers. He must look as tired as he felt.

"It's difficult, I know. But it's all worth it," his father said.

He didn't know what to say. This was not the time to voice any doubts, not with the guests in the living room. Maybe there would never be a time to voice any doubts to his father.

They oohed and aahed over the photos his parents had taken as well as those of Mira's parents. Theirs were pictures of the islands the ship had passed, the views of the glaciers from the helicopter and pictures of friends they'd met on the cruise. Then Matt brought his out. First the views of the eagles' nests from Carrie's plane. Then the town of Mystic, its houses, its school and the sound.

"It looks so small," his mother said, "and poor. What do the people do?"

"Population 350," he said. "The people fish and hunt and work in the store or teach at the school, what people do everywhere." He heard the defensive tone in his voice, but couldn't control it.

"They have no doctor, is that right?" Mira's father asked.

"That's why I went. There was a medical emergency." He showed the next slide. Carrie's face filled the screen. The picture he'd taken in her boat on the way to the island. Her hair was a vivid red-gold halo around her face. Her smile lit up the screen. She looked so vivacious, so alive, so real, so damned desirable, he felt as if he'd been struck by an arrow in the middle of his chest. He wished he'd never brought his slides. He wished he'd sorted through them first. There was a long silence in the room. He fumbled for the control so he could forward to the next slide, but he couldn't find the right button.

"Isn't that the young lady who came to the ship, the female pilot?" his father said. "The one who was so determined to get a doctor?"

"Yes," Matt said at last when he was able to speak. "That's Carrie." Finally he got to the next picture. Another one of Carrie, and then one of him in the boat that she'd taken. There were no pictures of her in the rain, or of her in the hot springs, or at her birthday party in her baggy coveralls, but that didn't keep the images from crowding his mind. He heard himself describing the town, the surrounding hills and the sound, but his voice seemed to belong to someone else. Somehow he got through the rest of them and he breathed a huge sigh of relief.

The conversation turned to other things besides their cruise. They talked of work and friends and neighbors. Matt hoped he was making appropriate comments while his mind spun around. He'd thought he would be able to forget her. He'd thought he'd be able to have a normal life without her, but right now he would be damned if he knew how to go about it. He was filled with the most intense longing he'd ever had in his life. Somehow he got through the evening. The guests left, and he was on his way out the door when his parents asked him about Mira.

"We're just friends," he said.

"I see," his mother said. "We had hoped…you seemed so right for each other."

"I know," he said. "But what it seemed was not what it was. I'm sorry to disappoint you."

"I'm sorry you had to disappoint Mira," she said. "She's such a lovely girl."

"Yes, she is," he agreed. "She deserves someone better than me. Good night."

He left them standing in the door, the expression on their faces puzzled concern.

When he got home he called Carrie again and left another message. He told her to page him at the hospital if he wasn't home, that he had to speak to her. The next day he went to the hospital and before he made rounds with the head of plastic surgery, he dropped in to see Jay, his friend in neurosurgery. He brought the slides he'd taken of Donny along with the latest information he'd gotten from Carrie.

Jay looked at the pictures and took the information that Carrie had sent Matt. He said he thought it was time to transport the patient. Matt explained his financial situation, and Jay said not to worry, there were funds for such patients and several of the doctors had volunteered to help out in these cases. He asked Matt about the transportation. Matt said he'd pay his way, that it would be arranged from up there.

He walked out of the office with a sense of purpose he'd lacked since his return from Alaska. Now if only he'd hear from Carrie so she could set things in motion. The hours dragged, the minutes lasted hours. She didn't call and she didn't call and he grew more restless than ever. Finally, when he was in the hospital cafeteria, forcing himself to eat a plateful of meat loaf and mashed potatoes before going back to work, his pager beeped. He snatched it up and saw her number on the screen. He jumped up from the table and found a quiet space outside in the staff parking lot where he called from his cell phone.

"How are you?" he demanded. "Where have you been?"

"Everywhere," she said. "I've never been so busy. How are you?"

He said he was fine, but he was far from fine. He was tense, he was nervous, he was so strung out he felt as if he was going to snap at any moment. "I'm busy, too. Look, from what you told me about Donny, the neurosurgeon thinks it may be time to bring him down. Can you do that?"

"I think so," she said. "I've found a guy who does medical evacuations regularly. I just have to see when he's free."

"I'll pay for it, whatever the cost," he said.

"I don't know if the family will accept charity," she said. "But I'll tell them you've offered."

"Tell them I insist," he said, knowing how poor they were. Knowing that Donny's father worked only seasonally at the zinc mine. "It will be good to see you." Good? It would be incredible, earth-shaking, amazing.

"Me? I don't think— There's no need— I mean, his mother or father will be coming with him. There's no reason for me to come."

His heart fell. "But I thought…" He'd always imagined her coming with him. He'd planned what they'd do together. They'd talked about it. Of course she'd demurred at the time, but by now he thought she might be missing him as much as he was missing her. He must be wrong. She didn't want to come.

"I understand," he said stiffly. "You're too busy. Well, let me know when you can schedule the plane."

Chapter Eleven

Carrie hung up the phone and sat down in a nearby chair with her whole body shaking uncontrollably. She had been proud of how fast her life got back to normal after Matt left. At least on the surface. She had a backlog of orders, of pickups and deliveries that kept her busy for days, flying out every morning and returning in the evening, exhausted and drained of all energy. She was glad for clear weather and for all the business. She didn't want time alone at home. She did not want to sit on the couch and gaze into the flames dancing in the fireplace by herself. She didn't want to cook for herself or eat by herself.

Deep down where it counted, she was disappointed that her life had not gotten back to normal. It was not normal for her to be bothered by the empty house or a table set for one. It was not normal for her to lie awake at night and think about what had been a strange and unusual interlude in her life. She was not one to dwell in the past. She'd gotten over a broken engagement and her father's death, and she would get over feeling let down because Matt had suddenly come into her life and then left just as abruptly.

She did her best not to think. During the day she was okay. When she was home, she checked up on Donny, took his vital signs the way Matt had taught her, took his blood pressure with the cuff he'd left behind, took his temperature with the digital thermometer he'd given her, checked his reflexes to see how much feeling had come back the way he'd shown her. Matt had said this next week would be crucial, so she knew he'd be checking with her and she wanted to have all the data when he called.

But when he'd first called, she was gone. The sound of his voice sent her pulse racing. She played the message over and over. She tried to call him back but he wasn't there. She hoped the conversation would be brief. She hoped that Donny would be the only topic of discussion. There was no point in talking about what had happened, or what might have happened or what could happen. It was over. Period. End of subject. She kept the information she'd gathered on Donny near the phone so she'd be ready. But she kept missing his calls.

Now that they'd finally connected, she wished they hadn't. Just the sound of his voice could make her break out in goose bumps all over her skin. She sat there for a long moment. Then she had a glass of wine. Then she walked around the house aimlessly, talking to herself. Warning herself, calming herself, telling herself he didn't feel the same as she did.

She had no intention of flying to San Francisco with Donny. He didn't need her along. One of his parents would go. If Carrie went it would be more painful than she was capable of bearing. She imagined seeing Matt at his hospital, surrounded by the latest technology and equipment, not to mention teams of specialists. She would quickly realize how out of place she was.

Then there was his family and his girlfriend. He'd said he was not going to marry her, but she had no idea if he'd changed his mind once he returned. No, Carrie was much better off where she was, busy, happy and content with the life she'd chosen. But had she chosen this life or had it been thrust on her? She'd had too much time to think these past days, too many hours in the plane, in a cloudless sky, too much time to ponder what she wanted from life.

She told herself that was enough introspection. It was time to get into action. She called the med-evac pilot then went to see Donny's family. They were nervous, scared and relieved at the same time. They peppered her with questions, most of which she couldn't answer.

Will they operate on him?

Will he be alone in the hospital?

How much will it cost?

Who will go with him?

The last one was settled quickly. His mother would go. But she wanted Carrie to go, too.

"Please, Carrie," Tillie asked. "I know it's a lot to ask, but I've never been farther than Juneau. I wouldn't know what to do, where to stay, how to get around."

Carrie couldn't ignore the troubled look in her eyes. She knew there was room in the plane. She knew it wouldn't cost any more if she went along. Yes, she had to go. But the same fears bothered her. Where would she stay? How would she get around?

What would she do? She kept these questions to herself and set the date for their departure for the next week.

"DAD," MATT SAID, "I need to talk to you."

His father took off his glasses, rubbed his eyes and sat back in his chair behind the large desk in his study. He only went to the hospital once or twice a week now, under orders from his doctor. Matt knew he hated to give up his practice but that he was now reading and writing about his field of reconstructive surgery on his new computer at home.

"What are you doing here?" Eugene asked with a glance at his watch. "I thought you made rounds today."

"Yes, usually. But..." Matt took a deep breath. What he was going to say was going to disappoint and hurt his father. He would give anything if he didn't have to tell him, but that wouldn't be fair, either. He wouldn't give his own life just so his father wouldn't be disappointed.

"I'm not going to do the internship," Matt said.

"What?" The pen flew out of his father's hand onto the floor. He stood and stared at Matt in disbelief. "But it's what you've always wanted. It's what you've planned and worked for. What happened?"

What happened. He needed to be as honest with his father as possible. And even more important, honest with himself.

"What happened is that I discovered that plastic surgery is not what I want to do."

"But you just began. You haven't given it a chance."

"I can't do it, Dad. I want to be a family doctor."

"Family doctor? Why?"

"For one thing I don't want to live in the city. I want to practice medicine in a small town somewhere."

"But you'd be setting broken bones and delivering babies and giving out cough syrup. You'd be bored in the first week."

"You may be right," Matt conceded, "but I don't think so. You remember that I did a rotation in family medicine once for three months. I loved it, but I never really considered doing it for good because, you know, I was committed to plastic surgery."

"I can't believe what I'm hearing," his father said, sitting down again.

"I knew you'd be disappointed. I'm disappointed, too," Matt said, taking a seat across from his father. "Disappointed that I can't follow in your footsteps. Disappointed to have to give up something I started. But when I went back up to Yuma last week and I saw the doctor I worked with and he offered me a job, I knew this was what I wanted to do. They're building a new hospital, and I ran into one of my patients who remembered me and I looked around and it just felt right to me the way plastic surgery has never felt right to me. As you remember, I passed out the first time I went into the O.R. with you."

"You were only sixteen," his father said. "And you haven't passed out since, have you?"

"No, but I've come close. I thought I'd get over it. I thought the rewards of seeing someone's life change because of the reconstruction I could do would be ample reward for becoming a surgeon, but it isn't. As for me, it's more than that. It's a lifestyle decision as much as anything else. I...I know it's difficult for you to understand, but I only hope you will. Maybe not now, but eventually.''

''Is there anything I can say to change your mind? Maybe you just need a break. Maybe you should wait till next year to start this internship. I'm sure I could put in a word, have them hold open your place for a year.''

''No, Dad, I don't want you to do that. I need to make my own decision. I have made my decision.''

His father nodded reluctantly. Then he drew his eyebrows together. ''Does this have anything to do with what happened up there in Alaska?''

''Yes, I think so. There, again, I was essentially practicing family medicine for a few days. Seeing all kinds of problems from broken legs to paralysis. In a small town, you get to know the people when they're sick and when they're well. You can treat the whole person. That's very appealing to me.''

''And that woman?'' his father continued.

Matt knew better than to play innocent and ask what woman? He knew and his father knew what woman.

''Yes, well, she is a wonderful woman. But I don't think I'll be seeing her again. She has a job up there, actually more than a job. She's a bush pilot, as you know, who inherited the business from her father. I don't see her ever leaving Alaska.'' Not even to visit San Francisco. Not even to come and see him. Not even to accompany the boy. He was hit once again by a sense of loss so profound he could only sit there frozen and stare unseeing at his father's framed diplomas on the wall.

"If she did leave…" his father said.

He shook his head. He didn't know what he'd do. Would he beg, plead or bribe her to give him a chance? Would it do any good?

"Do you love her?" his father asked, when he didn't answer.

Matt nodded. He loved her. He'd never told her but maybe she knew. Maybe that was why she refused to come down here with Donny. She didn't want to tell him she didn't love him.

Matt's gaze shifted to his father. The expression on his father's face had softened, as if he finally understood. What he didn't understand was that he had no idea if Carrie loved him. And if she did, did she love him enough to give up her life up there for him? If she didn't care enough to even come down here to see him, it was hopeless.

Matt stood up and so did his father. His father held out his arms, and Matt hugged him for the first time since he could remember. Eugene was not a demonstrative man. They were not an affectionate family. But something had happened today in this room. Matt's life was taking a new direction and maybe his relationship with his father was also taking one.

MATT WAS AT THE HELIPAD on the roof of the hospital waiting for the med-evac plane along with the paramedics. They wheeled Donny down the ramp on his gurney and he was relieved to see the boy smile. Matt greeted his mother and turned to follow the group when out of the corner of his eye he caught a glimpse of a tall, slim figure with red-gold hair gleaming in the California sunshine.

He whirled around, stood and stared, and she walked toward him. "You came."

"Yes," she said. "Tillie was afraid to come by herself. She's never been out of Alaska, you know, and so I thought, well, there's room in the plane, so…" She trailed off.

If he thought she'd come to see him, she was taking pains to let him know that wasn't the case. It had nothing to do with him. It was all about helping Donny's family. Of course it was. But he couldn't help the hope that surged inside him. The thoughts that crowded his mind. Maybe…just maybe…

Matt saw that Donny got settled in his room and that he was being given a thorough exam. Matt told his mother he'd reserved a room for her in the house for patients' parents. She thanked him but he could see she wasn't ready to leave her son's side just yet. Matt's friend the neurosurgeon would be by later.

Matt took Carrie aside in the hall outside Donny's room.

"This is wonderful, what you've done," she said in a low voice. "I'm overwhelmed by all the attention he's getting."

"This is just the beginning," he said. "It may take a while. First the tests, then the diagnosis, then the decision about what will be done. If it's surgery, we're talking about a long recovery time."

"Yes, I see." She looked thoughtful. "I don't know how long his mother can stay. She has the other children back home."

"And you?" he asked.

"I didn't know how long we'd be here so I can-
celed some of my orders. I guess I can stay as long
as they need me."

"What about me?" he asked. He shouldn't have
asked her that now. Not now when she'd just arrived,
and certainly not here in the busy hallway with the
loudspeaker paging certain doctors and aides rushing
by with trays of medicines. He should have waited.
But suddenly he couldn't wait any longer. He'd been
waiting all his life for her and she was here, in person,
her face, her amber eyes looking at him so intently,
her lips parted as if she was going to say something,
something that would change his life.

Before she could speak, his friend Jay arrived and
was introduced to everyone. Then Jay asked that the
room be cleared so he could do an exam. Matt took
Carrie and Tillie down to the coffee shop and ordered
sandwiches and coffee for them. He asked about
everyone he'd met in Mystic, and they told him everything that had happened, all the gossip and all the
news from the small town. But Carrie didn't answer
the questions he had to have an answer to. What about
me? Will you stay as long as I need you? Will you
stay forever? Do you love me?

He didn't have a chance to ask her any of these
questions until that evening. Until after they'd settled
Donny and his mother. Until they'd made sure they'd
both been given dinner and Tillie knew where she
was staying. He told Carrie the room for Tillie was
in a special residence for family members of patients.
He told Carrie—rather than asked her—that she
would stay with him in his apartment. He thought she
might object, but she just nodded. He felt a rush of

relief. Once he had her alone he could say what he wanted to say. But he didn't. If the answers to his questions were no, he didn't think he could take it.

CARRIE LOOKED AROUND at Matt's apartment with its new beige carpet and buttery leather sofa and was struck by the contrast to her own house furnished with odds and ends collected over the years. It was more clear than ever to her how different they were. Too different.

He put her suitcase in his bedroom that was furnished with a large bed with a natural, light-colored wood frame and matching dresser.

"Wait," she said. "I'll sleep on the couch."

"Not in my house," he said firmly.

"But in my house…"

"You make the rules, but here…"

She gave him a faint smile and gave in. She was so tired and so tense, after the stress of getting Donny safely into the plane in Mystic, the long flight down and then seeing Matt. When she got off the plane her heart raced and she kept her hands clenched into fists. He looked even better than she'd remembered. So calm and competent and so very handsome in his white coat with his name pinned to his lapel. M. Baker, M.D.

She'd imagined that moment so many times. She imagined throwing herself into his arms, telling him how much she'd missed him. That was in her dreams. In reality there were so many people around, so many more important things to do than indulge in her fantasy. Even if they'd been alone, she wouldn't have said anything except she was glad to see him. Glad?

That was the understatement of the year. She was excited, terrified, numb, breathless and more.

She shouldn't have been surprised to find that he looked so at home here in the city, that he fitted in so well at the big-city hospital. It was still a shock to realize once again that he belonged here and she belonged there.

"I want to take you out to dinner," he said. "I want to show you the town."

She shook her head. She had no energy to see the town and no clothes to see it in. "Not tonight," she said. "I'm too tired. Besides, don't you have to get up early or be on call or something?"

"No."

That was all he said, but he said it so firmly she gave him a quizzical look, which he ignored. She wanted to ask why not. She wanted to ask what his schedule was, but she didn't. She asked how the internship was going, and he said that was a long story. Then he changed the subject.

"I can't offer you any homemade soup, but I could call out for a pizza," he said.

"With mushrooms and anchovies? I'd love that. You may have noticed, there's no pizza in Mystic. Dried fish yes, pizza no."

They ate the pizza in the living room, sitting on the floor around his Swedish Modern coffee table. Carrie savored every bite and sipped the undoubtedly expensive wine he poured for her.

He slanted a smile in her direction. "Glad to see you haven't lost your appetite."

"Was I gobbling? I didn't mean to. I thought I wasn't hungry, but I guess I was," she said, wiping her mouth with a napkin. "I haven't had a pizza since I don't know…months, years. I could get used to—" She stopped abruptly hoping he hadn't heard or noticed. He had.

"Get used to what?" he asked, leveling his gaze at her across the table. "Calling out for food when you're too tired to cook? Or get used to living with me?"

"Matt," she said, setting her glass down. What did he expect from her? Why did he even ask?

"Never mind," he said, holding up his hand. "Forget I said that. You just got here. I didn't mean to put you on the spot."

She nodded, but she couldn't forget what he'd said. When he went to the kitchen to make coffee, she stood up and looked out the window. His apartment looked out on a busy street. It was convenient to the hospital and to a large park on the other side of the street. But the noise and the lights and the frantic pace were so alien to her she could never get used to living in such a place, not after growing up in a small Alaska village. She was glad he'd withdrawn his question.

She was afraid she wouldn't be able to sleep. She thought she'd feel guilty about Matt on the couch. She thought she'd be too tense or too worried about Donny, but after Matt ran a bath for her in the extra-long tub, she put her old flannel granny gown on and paused for a moment in the doorway to the living room where Matt was sitting on the couch reading. It was like the nights at her house and yet it wasn't. In some ways this place he lived in was like another planet.

But when she saw him there, one arm stretched

along the back of the sofa, she had the strangest feeling that she'd come home. Here, in a place so much the antithesis of her real home that she was baffled. Yet it was undeniable. The sight of Matt sitting on a couch, the lamplight on his head made her feel that she belonged there.

She had an unbearable urge to tell him that if he asked her, she'd live here in this noisy city with him. If he loved her, she'd give up her business, her town and her friends, because without him, without love, all those things faded away and became meaningless. She wanted to slide up next to him, to feel his arm around her, her hip next to his. That was all it would take and she would know she belonged there, in his arms, wherever he was, wherever he lived. She held her breath, waiting, hoping, praying…

He looked up, and in the light from his reading lamp, his eyes appeared so dark they were fathomless. He didn't say anything, but she felt his gaze travel the length of her nightgown. The heat from his gaze sent a flame through her body, so hot she felt scorched. She was breathing hard, as if she'd run all the way from Mystic. For a long while their eyes held, the bond between them so strong she could almost feel it stretch between them. But he didn't speak. He didn't ask the question she had the answer to. Without the question, she couldn't give the answer. She couldn't say the words she wanted to say. Finally he said good-night, and she went to his bedroom and closed the door behind her.

Under his comforter, in his bed, between his sheets, she fell asleep at last.

In the morning they went to the hospital. Jay met

them outside Donny's room. He was holding the results of some of the tests. Today they would do a CAT scan and an MRI. It would be a few days before they decided on a course of treatment. He told them he was hopeful that Donny would recover completely.

Then Carrie and Matt went into Donny's room and spoke to him and his mother. Tillie was having her meals at the table next to his bed. In between, she read or watched TV with her son. She seemed in good spirits, cheered by the optimistic attitude of the doctor and the kindness of the nurses. She had no desire to leave the hospital grounds.

Matt said he was going to take Carrie on a ride out of town. Tillie smiled and told them to have a good time. When they left the hospital Carrie asked where they were going.

"A small town in the foothills of the Sierras. So you won't think all of California is like this." He waved his hand at the line of buses and cars, at the fumes and the noise in the street. "It's the least I can do after you took me all over in your boat. It's the place I told you about, the town where I did the residency in family medicine."

"Will we be back tonight or shall I get my suitcase?"

"It's a few hours' drive each way. We'll come back tonight."

The hours flew by. The awkwardness of the day before was gone. The tension of the evening had disappeared. He described the crops that grew in the fields along the road, explained the meaning of the Spanish or Indian place names. She asked questions, but not the ones she wanted most to know the answer to.

Do you love me?

What do you want of me?

At one point he put his hand on her knee and said, "I'm glad you came." Maybe that's all she would get. Maybe she'd have to settle for that. Maybe she'd have to go home and face life without him.

She turned to face him. "So am I," she said. But that was all.

The town was charming. Matt told her it was once a gold-mining town, as was Mystic. He told something of the colorful characters who founded it, then showed her their graves in the small cemetery up the hill.

"Pickard, Jones, Wilton," he read from the tombstones. "The first families of Yuma. Then and now. There are still quite a few of them in town."

"You know a lot about the town."

"I know they have a nice library."

"I suppose it's a little bigger than ours."

"Yes, it is. So big I hear they need help."

She shot a quick glance in his direction. What did that have to do with anything?

"How long were you here?" she asked, stooping over to pick a dandelion between graves.

"Three months, but it seemed longer," he said gazing down the hill at the small houses clustered around the town square. "Not because I didn't like it, I did. Time goes slower up here. But you know that, coming from a small town yourself."

"Mystic makes this town look like New York."

He leaned against the wooden fence that bordered the cemetery. "I have to tell you something, Carrie."

Here it comes, she thought. He's getting married. I should have known. That's why he hasn't said anything.

She tried to say something but her throat was too dry.

"I'm not going to be a plastic surgeon."

"What?"

He gave her a rueful smile. "That's exactly what my father said… 'What?'"

"What happened?" she said when she finally found her voice.

He waited a long moment while he looked at the graves around him. "I came up here a little while ago, to the town, to this cemetery, and it caused me to think about my future. For some time I've pretended that plastic surgery was what I wanted. Maybe because I wanted to want it. Maybe because my father wanted it for me.

"But also it was the time I spent here and then the time I spent in Mystic with you. Small town, general medicine. It's the kind of medicine I like and the way of life I want. There's just one thing missing. You."

She was stunned. She couldn't believe it. "Me?" Her voice cracked on that one little word.

"I know, I know. You have your own life, your own house, your town. You don't need me. But think about me. Think about how much I need you. I thought I could get along without you. I thought I could forget you. But I can't. I don't know what I can say to persuade you to give up everything you have, to marry me and live here with me and raise our children here.''

Her mind spun around. She was dizzy, delirious. *Marry me, raise our children...* Did he really say those words or had she just imagined them? ''How about 'I love you'?'' she asked breathlessly and to the point.

''That's it?'' he asked, grabbing her around the waist and lifting her in the air. ''Just 'I love you'?''

She laughed out loud with joy and relief in the clear, quiet air. ''That's it,'' she said, ''Just 'I love you, I love you, I love you.'''

Epilogue

The wedding was held in Carrie's house in Mystic. The whole village was invited and most of them came, crowding into the living room, the kitchen and filling the hallway. There was even a large crowd who had to stand on the front porch. Carrie watched them all arrive from her bedroom window upstairs. When she saw Donny walk slowly up the front steps with his family, she breathed a prayer of thanks. He'd made a miraculous recovery since returning from San Francisco. The new nurse was there, too, the one who'd answered the ad they put in the nursing magazine. She was a hardy, adventurous soul who was looking forward to life in the village and who would rent Carrie's house and boat from her. Carrie had sold the business to a man in Nome who'd come down to get her plane next week. Signing the papers hadn't been easy, but she thought her father would understand. He'd raised her to think for herself and make her own decisions. He knew they wouldn't all be easy.

Carrie's father's best friend, Russ, was in the living room rehearsing his lines so he could perform the ceremony by the power invested in him by the State of Alaska, just as he'd assured her father he would.

Matt's parents were there. She'd flown them in from Juneau yesterday, and they were staying with Merry and her husband until tomorrow. They'd been such good sports, hiding their surprise when they saw how small and primitive the town was. They called it charming and rustic. They'd actually been amazingly kind to her, from the moment Matt broke the news to them, considering they'd had other plans for their son that didn't include her or his change in career.

Carrie wore a white dress she'd bought in San Francisco with Matt's mother's help. She walked down the stairs while the wedding march was played on a fiddle by an old-timer who'd learned from his father.

Matt stood in front of the fireplace waiting for her. He watched her walk slowly toward him, her gaze locked on his and his heart filled with joy. Tears stung her eyes, tears of joy. Her only regret was that her father couldn't be there to give her away. She knew he'd be happy to know about her wedding, about Matt and about how much she loved him. Maybe he did know. Maybe he was rejoicing somewhere.

It was a short, traditional ceremony, and afterward everyone went to the school gym for the reception. It was a bit like her birthday party, only this time she was prepared and dressed for the occasion. The high school band played, and everyone danced, old and young. The newlyweds were the first couple on the floor to start the dancing. Matt held her in his arms and led her around the polished floor of the basketball court.

"Did you ever think that day we were running back and forth on these boards that one day we'd be dancing on the same floor?" she asked.

He shook his head and held her close. "Dancing with you was the farthest thing from my mind," he said. "But marrying you? That was something I wanted to do from the first moment I saw you. I just never thought it would happen. You said you were never lonely."

"I wasn't, until I met you."

"I heard you were completely self-sufficient."

"I was, until I met you."

"No regrets about leaving all this behind, selling the plane and giving up your career?" He knew the answer. He just wanted to hear it again.

"It wasn't my career, it was my dad's. Just like plastic surgery wasn't yours, either. We both found what we wanted."

"I wanted you," he murmured in her ear.

"You have me," she answered softly. "For as long as we both shall live."

HARLEQUIN®

AMERICAN *Romance*®

Celebrate 20 Years
of Home, Heart and Happiness!

Join us for a yearlong anniversary celebration as we
bring you not-to-be-missed miniseries such as:

MILLIONAIRE, MONTANA

A small town wins a huge jackpot in this six-book continuity
(January–June 2003)

THE BABIES OF DOCTORS CIRCLE

Jacqueline Diamond's darling doctor trilogy
(March, May, July 2003)

A ROYAL
TWIST

Victoria Chancellor's witty royal duo
(January and February 2003)

And look for your favorite authors throughout the year, including:

Muriel Jensen's JACKPOT BABY (January 2003)

Judy Christenberry's
SAVED BY A TEXAS-SIZED WEDDING (May 2003)

Cathy Gillen Thacker's brand-new
DEVERAUX LEGACY story (June 2003)

Look for more exciting programs throughout the year
as Harlequin American Romance celebrates its 20th Anniversary!

Available at your favorite retail outlet.

HARLEQUIN®
Makes any time special®

Visit us at www.eHarlequin.com

HARTAC

Coming in February 2003 from

HARLEQUIN®

AMERICAN *Romance*®

BIG-BUCKS BACHELOR
by
Leah Vale

The latest book in the scintillating six-book series,

MILLIONAIRE, MONTANA

Welcome to Millionaire, Montana, where twelve lucky townspeople have won a multimillion-dollar jackpot. And where one millionaire in particular has just...
caught himself a fake fiancée.

MILLIONAIRE, MONTANA continues with

SURPRISE INHERITANCE
by Charlotte Douglas,
on sale March 2003.

Available at your favorite retail outlet.

HARLEQUIN®
Makes any time special®

**Start the New Year off regally with
a two-book duo from**

HARLEQUIN®

AMERICAN *Romance*®

*A runaway prince and his horse-wrangling
lookalike confuse and confound
the citizens of Ranger Springs, Texas, in*

♛A ROYAL
TWIST
by
Victoria Chancellor

Rodeo star Hank McCauley just happened to be a dead ringer
for His Royal Highness Prince Alexi of Belegovia—who had just
taken off from his tour of Texas with a spirited, sexy waitress.
Now, Hank must be persuaded by the very prim-and-proper
Lady Gwendolyn Reed to pose as the prince until the lost leader
is found. But could she turn the cowpoke into a Prince
Charming? And could Hank persuade Lady "Wendy" to let
down her barriers so that he could have her, body and soul?

Don't miss:

THE PRINCE'S COWBOY DOUBLE
January 2003

Then read Prince Alexi's story in:

THE PRINCE'S TEXAS BRIDE
February 2003

Available at your favorite retail outlet.

HARLEQUIN®
Makes any time special ®

HARLEQUIN

AMERICAN *Romance*

Bestselling author
Muriel Jensen
kicks off

MILLIONAIRE, MONTANA

beginning in January 2003 with
JACKPOT BABY

Welcome to Millionaire, Montana, where twelve lucky
townspeople have won a multimillion-dollar jackpot.
And where one millionaire in particular has just…
found a baby on her doorstep.

The excitement continues with:

BIG-BUCKS BACHELOR by Leah Vale
on-sale February 2003

SURPRISE INHERITANCE by Charlotte Douglas
on-sale March 2003

FOUR-KARAT FIANCÉE by Sharon Swan
on-sale April 2003

PRICELESS MARRIAGE by Bonnie Gardner
on-sale May 2003

FORTUNE'S TWINS by Kara Lennox
on-sale June 2003

Available at your favorite retail outlet.